"Doubt thou the stars are fire,
Doubt that the sun doth move,
Doubt truth to be a liar,
But never doubt I love."

Hamlet
William Shakespeare.

The Navigation Quartet

1: Veering Off Course

Veering off Course

The Navigation Quartet

1: Veering Off Course

Chris Cheek

2FM Limited

Consultancy and Analysis
Publishing & Communication

**Rossholme, West End, Long Preston
Skipton, North Yorkshire, BD23 4QL**

Tel: 01729 840756
e-mail: admin@two-fm.co.uk

Cover images: Shutterstock, David Burrell

A CIP catalogue record for this book is available
from the British Library

ISBN 978-1-9996479-4-0

With grateful thanks
and best wishes
Chris Chell

Dedication

For Gill and Mark Thomas
Here's to more than 40 years of friendship.
You gave me my lift to London, Mark, and I am forever grateful.

Prologue

Sedgethwaite, West Yorkshire.

February 1997.

Alan Foreshaw and David Edgeley were both nineteen. They had been close friends for years – they'd met on Alan's first day at their junior school aged nine. Since then, they had done everything together – gone fishing, shoplifted a couple of small items, chatted up girls, conned pub landlords into thinking they were over age – and each lost their virginity, simultaneously and in adjacent rooms in a Blackpool boarding house. Alan was pretty much the only close friend that David had ever had, though he was also close to Mona, who had been in their class at school.

And now Alan was leaving. He had always been the more adventurous one, and he'd gone and got himself a job in London. David had swapped his rest day so that they could have a farewell night out – a few drinks in the old haunts, see some mates, perhaps even pick up a couple of girls. He wanted to give Alan a last night to remember in Sedgethwaite, the Yorkshire mill town in which they'd grown up.

It was gone eleven now, and the pubs were shutting. They'd ended up in the Boot and Shoe in the town centre. The bar was packed, as it was most nights, mostly with people they knew from drinking in here – legally and illegally – ever since they could at least pass for eighteen. There were a few familiar faces from school. Couples and several pairings of girls together, out for a good time and maybe to meet some boys. Alan and David waved and exchanged greetings with several people during the evening, but they'd been much too busy drinking and talking to bother about the girls. Several had eyed them speculatively as they sat close together at a corner table. Apart from anything else, the night had seemed too important to spoil by wasting time with other people.

As the landlord called time, the two boys emerged onto the street. Sedgethwaite's town centre was busy as all the pubs reached chucking-out time. The weather was dry now but it had only just stopped raining, leaving the streets wet and buildings still dripping. Looking down the long slope of the High Street, they could see the reflections of the blue street lights in the pavements as the stone buildings echoed to the laughter and some shouting from the revellers now headed home. A late bus came up from the bus station, announced by the hiss of its tyres on the wet road surface. As it neared them, they could hear the beat of its windscreen wipers, still moving to deal with residual spray. Then it was past them and going on up the hill, the sound of its engine reverberating against the shops and offices.

Clubbing together just before closing time, David and

Alan raised enough cash to buy half a bottle of scotch and they walked slowly back to Alan's place to drink it. He lived with his Auntie Mary and she was already in bed; she was a bit deaf anyway, meaning that they would be left alone.

They fetched glasses and settled down on the sitting-room floor. In the fuggy heat from the gas fire, they drank the scotch and reminisced about their times together.

"Do you remember our day out on Ilkley Moor?" asked Alan at one point.

"Aye, was that the time you trod in a cow pat?"

"That's the one. In above my bloody ankle I went. Stank all the way home."

David laughed. "God, yes. We had half the bus to ourselves 'cos nobody wanted to sit near us. I don't know how I managed to stay with you."

"Guilty conscience, I expect."

"Guilty? Me? Why was that, then?"

"Because you'd pushed me."

"I did not."

"You did too – we were chasing that tennis ball we found and you fouled me."

"Referee! That was a fair shoulder charge! It were no foul – well, at least not until you stepped in summat. That was certainly foul!"

"Oh ha bloody ha. You bugger." There was no anger in Alan's tone, though. He grinned at his pal. "We've had some good times, though – especially that weekend in Blackpool. What were they called? Sharon and Tracey?"

"God, I remember that – they were all over us on the back seat before we'd even got on to the motorway. By the time we got there, I was so turned on I thought I'd die."

"Yeah, Sharon had a wicked tongue I seem to remember."

David laughed, "Aye, in all senses of the word. A voice like a foghorn as well. We were staying near Central Pier, I seem to remember."

"That's right. Just two streets back from the prom."

"Aye, Mrs Morgan, wasn't it?"

"Well, not only did Mrs Morgan know we were at it, the whole of central Blackpool must have heard Sharon."

Alan smiled at the memory, though a shadow flitted across his face. His own time with Tracey had been a bit more difficult. He'd managed something eventually, but he could never claim to have enjoyed the night – in fact, it was his only time ever with a girl.

The whisky had run out by now, and the flood of reminiscence slowed to a trickle. They both became drowsy. David realised that he was cradling Alan's head in his lap. It happened sometimes during these late-night talks as they stretched out close together but tonight, somehow, it felt different.

Tentatively David reached out and touched his friend's forehead. Alan had always been there, always been central to his existence. How was he going to cope without him? How would he get through every day without the knowledge that Alan was there, waiting for him?

"Are you asleep, Al?"

There was no reply. Looking down at Alan's face, David had a strange feeling. He had experienced something similar a couple of times before, but somehow the moment had never been right. Now, well...

Trembling slightly, he reached out and stroked Alan's

hair. Then he leant forward and kissed him on the forehead.

Alan opened his eyes and smiled. "You'll never know how long I've waited for that, Davy." He sat up and kissed David on the lips. They embraced and kissed again. "Come up to bed."

For a moment, David hesitated, wondering what was going to happen and what it would mean. But this was Al, his biggest mate. Nothing could be wrong about Al. He followed his friend up the stairs. Once there, they undressed quietly, stealing kisses between shedding garments, shushing each other so as to not to waken Alan's aunt. Once naked, they lay together on the bed, legs entwined, kissing and holding each other tightly.

Lying close to Alan and wrapped in his arms was the most beautiful sensation David had ever felt. Eventually, their passion rose; Alan arranged them so that their erections rubbed together and wrapped his fist round them both. They began to thrust, gently at first, but then with an accelerating rhythm. They reached their climaxes with seconds of each other. For both of them, it was an earth-shattering moment.

Afterwards they lay together, kissing gently once more, recovering their breath and coming down from the high they had just experienced. Alan cleaned them both up with some tissues and they rearranged themselves for sleep, still holding each other close.

Alan went out like a light but David lay awake, watching his friend sleep. What had just happened? And why now, when Alan was about to leave? It was the most pure, the most exhilarating, the most meaningful experience of his life. But it was wrong. It was so wrong... And what about the future? How was he supposed to do without his constant companion and childhood friend? Alan's departure was going to leave a gap in his life that he had not known for nigh on ten years. Being on his own and coping with what had just happened: it was almost too much to bear.

His brain felt like a wasps' nest – a jumble of unconnected thoughts and speculation, all buzzing around, each demanding his attention. After a few minutes, he made a conscious effort to empty his mind and to try to sleep. Finally he succeeded.

Alan woke early when he heard the first signs of Auntie Mary moving about. He shook David awake and kissed him long and hard, but neither spoke as David dressed hurriedly.

Ready to go, David kissed Alan again and then found the words he wanted. "Don't go to London. Stay with me, Al. Please?"

Alan shook his head. "I have to go, Davy, especially after this. I've known for a long time, you see, at least about me. I've got to get away from here." He paused and then said, "You could always come with me, you know."

David felt a stab of fear and shook his head. "Couldn't really."

Alan smiled sadly. David's reaction was what he had expected: he had always been the careful one in their friendship. "Actually, you could. But I thought you wouldn't. Now, goodbye, Davy, and good luck."

When David got home, his mother was just getting breakfast. She was amused by his somewhat bedraggled appearance. "You had a good night, then," she remarked.

David grinned. "Aye, we were three sheets to t'wind, so

I stayed at Alan's – I slept on the floor."

The lie came easily and brought him up short. Why had he said that? Why had he not just said "I stayed with Alan"? It was by no means the first time he'd slept over. Was this the start of the lies and deception he would have to practise if he did turn out to be queer? He shivered at the thought.

"Do you want some breakfast?"

"No, thanks. I'll go up and get my head down for a couple of hours, if you don't mind."

Once upstairs, the turmoil he had felt during the night resurfaced. Kissing Alan, going to bed with him – how could he even begin to describe how it had felt to hold Alan in his arms? Certainly no experience with a woman had come close. But then he felt a shiver of fear; what would it mean for him, stuck here in Sedgethwaite?

There was one guy at the depot, Gerry, a clerk in the office, who was quite effeminate in his behaviour and was openly gay. On the surface at least, Gerry coped quite well with the ribbing he got from his older colleagues, but there had been the odd occasion when David had noticed him wince when remarks got a bit close to the bone. The worst bit was that David was also in a position to hear what was said about Gerry behind his back, and that was not very nice at all.

He wasn't a fool. He read the papers and watched television: he knew how much British society had always hated queers, how the police had often targeted them and hooligans bashed them up. Things had changed, obviously – the age of consent had been reduced, and discrimination was being tackled. But changing the law didn't always change people's minds, particularly not in a small town like Sedgethwaite. Judging by the conversations he overhead the pub and the canteen, attitudes had hardly shifted at all. Well, he certainly wasn't getting involved with any of that.

If Alan had still been around, if they'd been able to face it together, it might have been different. But that was not going to happen – Alan was going to London. Last night had happened and couldn't be undone. But it must not happen again.

✥

The weeks following Alan's departure flew by. Down in London, Alan found a flat and sent David a note of his new address and phone number. He spent some weeks hoping for a letter or a card in reply but received nothing. Eventually, he gave up hoping and got on with his new life.

In Sedgethwaite, David remained resolute. He made a plan and followed it through. As a result, the next time he contacted Alan was three months later when he sent him an invitation to his wedding: he was marrying Mona.

Alan did not respond.

Chapter 1

David, six years later

David Edgeley shut the front door quietly and set off down the hill. The pavements glistened with frost and he shivered slightly in the pre-dawn cold. The view from his estate was spectacular: the West Yorkshire mill town of Sedgethwaite lay stretched out in the valley below, the streetlamps blinking in the cold air. Rows of terraced houses lined the streets, which acted like tendrils, merging and flowing together down towards the vast woollen mills – many now decaying and derelict – that stood next to the river as it snaked through the landscape in the valley bottom.

David noticed the steam from his breath and hoped that old Jim, the staff bus driver, was running on time. Still shivering, he arrived at the stop and cursed himself, not for the first time, for having a daft job that meant getting up at four-thirty in the morning. Still, he would be finished by dinnertime and, if the skies stayed clear, he might get some gardening done in the afternoon. Anyway, he'd been on the buses for nearly seven years now, since he was eighteen, and he couldn't see himself going back into a factory.

A distant growl announced that Jim was coaxing one of the older buses up the hill to the 1930s' council estate where David lived. He glanced at his watch: only a couple of minutes late – not bad. The bus appeared around the corner, the noise of the straining engine reverberating around the houses.

"Morning, Jim."

"Hello, David, lad. How's tha doin'?"

"Bloody cold."

"Aye, there is a nip this morning."

David sat down and they set off. There were muttered greetings from the dozen passengers already aboard, closely followed by a yell from the back of the bus. "Hello, lover boy!"

"Morning, Pat," he responded warily.

"Are you cold, then, love?"

"Aye, bloody cold."

"Ooh, shall I come and warm you up?"

David winced. Pat Eckersley was one of company's growing band of women drivers, a stunner in her day, who, it was rumoured, had enjoyed the favours of many of her colleagues at the depot during her long career – and quite possibly a good few passengers as well.

Despite being fairly short at five foot seven, David was solidly built with dark brown hair and boyish good looks. This meant that most of the women had mothered him since he first joined the company, but Pat had other ideas. She'd got no response, though, and resorted instead to some very bawdy banter. He was used to it now, but it had been a source of acute embarrassment to him over the years, particularly in the early days of his marriage to Mona.

"Well, lover boy? I'm waiting!"

"No thanks, Pat, love. I'll have to make do with a nice cup of Bovril today."

There was laughter from the rest of the staff, after which they all went quiet as they tried to come to terms with the start of another day. The silence survived, apart from muttered greetings to a few newcomers, until they reached their destination.

At the depot, they all piled out and into the office to greet the depot inspector. The building, like many depots around the country, had been built in the heyday of the industry in the 1930s and little had changed since. Polished concrete floors, gloss-painted walls in institutional brown and cream, and a distinctive odour: a mix of raw diesel, exhaust fumes, hot oil and fried food. David felt at home every day as soon as he inhaled it.

"Morning, Jack."

"Morning, young David. What are you on then?"

"First Leeds – twenty-two duty."

"Oh, aye. Here's your board – you've got 733."

"One of the new ones. Hey, not bad!"

"Look after it, lad – they're too bloody expensive to go buggering about with."

"I will, don't you worry."

Jack Davis smiled. When you'd been a depot inspector for fifteen years, you knew who your reliable staff were. Young Edgeley had never failed for an early turn yet, and already had three safe-driving diplomas under his belt. A steady lad – the highest compliment in Jack's vocabulary.

✛

It was said of the Sedgethwaite to Leeds service that all you needed to do was run a bus up and down the road and you could it fill it at any time of the day or night. Whether or not that was true, it was certainly the best used service in the company's network.

Even at five-thirty in the morning, there were a good twenty people waiting as David pulled onto his stand in the bus station refreshed by a quick cuppa before leaving the depot. Most of the passengers were regulars, and there were brief greetings as they bought their tickets.

The road to Leeds was a classic example of pre-war ribbon development, with small villages dribbling into each other along the main road. There was very little traffic at such an early hour, which meant that David had to watch his time. He was keenly aware that leaving stops ahead of schedule was the bus driver's greatest sin, especially that early in the morning.

The bus he was driving was very new indeed, having only entered service the previous month. He could not help but smile when he compared the sophistication of the power steering and automatic gearbox with his grandad's stories of bus driving just after the war: tales of starting handles, crash gearboxes and steering that was as likely to slip you a disc as take you round a corner. It was a different world today, though probably a less happy one; there'd been a bus every two minutes on the Sedgethwaite–Leeds route in those days.

The journey was largely uneventful; one man's season ticket had run out and he was made to pay his fare. He accused David of 'havin' shares in t' bloody company', but it was all fairly good humoured.

The bus drew into Leeds Bus Station at 0614, dead on time. Passengers off, handbrake on, engine off, note the number of tickets sold, and over to the canteen for another quick cuppa. It was just beginning to get light. Another day had properly begun.

✛

The skies stayed clear, so David was able to set to in the garden after a bite of dinner and a doze.

Every now and again the settled nature of his life worried him; the pattern seemed set for the next forty years. Since there did not seem to be much he could do about it, he usually dismissed the thought – and besides it wasn't really true. He and Mona were saving to buy their own house and there were the boys to be fed, clothed and brought up. Seeing them through school and safely into adulthood, now that was surely challenge enough for anybody.

He returned to his weeding and smiled at his younger son, Kevin, busy trying to help. At the age of three, there could be precious few worries in his mind about the future. Mona was in the kitchen, just putting the kettle on. Of medium height, with long straight brown hair, she was quite an attractive girl even if, as she was the first to admit, she was not pretty enough to have guaranteed as good a catch as David for a husband.

In fact, they had lived in the same road as kids and had been pals since they'd started school at the age of four. Despite that, David's offer of marriage had taken her by surprise; they had drifted apart around the time Alan left for London. As a result, the proposal had come out of the blue. Mona was flattered, and she certainly wasn't going to refuse. Even so, had anybody asked she would have been hard put to find a convincing answer as to why she'd married him. It had just felt right, that was all.

However, she was happy enough now not to bother about such things – and certainly happier than either her mother or her mother-in-law admitted to. There was only one fly in the ointment. They seemed to count their husbands' lack of sexual interest as a positive bonus; Mona was less sure. She'd have welcomed a bit more interest on David's part. From what she read and saw on television, regular sex was part and parcel of everyone's life. Not in their household, though. It had been a good few weeks since... And he did look rather sexy in those old gardening jeans. She dismissed the thought and brewed the tea.

"Cup of tea, love?"

"Aye, thanks. It's nearly time to collect young Tommy from school, isn't it?" Their elder son was five and had started school just after Christmas.

"Yes, but you've time for a cuppa."

✥

Later, the boys fed and safely in bed, they sat down in front of the television. With David on early turn it would be a short evening; they would be in bed by ten at the latest.

Mona sat impassively, absorbed by a soap opera, but David was restless.

"What a load of bloody rubbish."

"Well, I like it," his wife replied. "It's true to life."

"How would you know? You've never been to America."

"I know, but it seems true. Don't watch it if you don't want to. Go down the road for a pint."

"No, I'm too tired. Anyway, you know I don't like that place."

Mona sighed. "I don't know. You're a funny lad, David Edgeley."

"What do you mean?"

"You've always been the same. Never bothered with the lads much."

"That's not true. I'm just not that fond of beer. Any road, all they ever talk about is football and sex. It gets bloody boring. I'd much rather read a book – it's cheaper, too!"

"Go on, read one then."

"I can't concentrate with this on."

"I'll turn it off."

"Don't be daft, lass. I'll survive."

They lapsed into silence and watched the rest of the programme, but the discussion was resumed as they got ready for bed.

"I don't know what's the matter with you lately," said Mona.

David frowned. "What do you mean?"

"You always seem so restless. Aren't you happy?"

"Aye, happy enough," he replied noncommittally.

"I don't know, then. But there's something up with you."

"Don't be daft."

They got into bed. Mona's remarks worried David; he knew he was feeling restless, but he'd not realised it was that obvious. It didn't mean anything. He grinned at his wife. "Perhaps it's the spring coming early."

"Go on with you," Mona replied, snuggling up to him and reaching inside his pyjamas.

David froze. Sensing his reaction, she moved away, giving him a quick peck on the cheek and sighing slightly. "Good night, love," she said.

"I'm on early turn."

"I know. Forget it. Night-night."

Chapter 2

Alan

Alan Foreshaw awoke to the klaxon-like sounds of his bedside alarm clock. He hated the noise with a passion, and regularly promised himself either to change the tone or throw the bloody thing out. He hadn't carried out either resolution because he knew that it was the only thing that would wake him up every day.

He hit the snooze button, giving him three- or four-minutes' respite before it went off again. Then he really would have to get up. He had an important client meeting at ten and he had to be there on time.

He still marvelled at the luck that had landed him the job he was now doing. He was an account manager in a medium-sized advertising agency, having risen through the ranks from junior office boy, the post he had originally secured to get a toehold in London six years earlier.

In his mid-teens when he was still at school, he'd felt the draw of life in the capital because it seemed much more glamourous than Sedgethwaite, the West Yorkshire town in which he had been brought up. There was another reason too, a more important one: his sexuality. Growing up as a gay man, he had known that life in his home town would be restrictive and difficult. Far better to seek the opportunities offered by a big city and its anonymity.

He and the advertising business had clicked from day one and his rise through the ranks had been rapid, especially for someone who had left school at the age of sixteen with only the basic five GSCEs. He had studied hard since, of course, and had already done his Institute of Marketing exams. Now he was part way through a marketing degree at the Open University. After that, an MBA course might beckon if he did well enough.

Meanwhile a combination of good looks, personal charm, project-management skills and an instinctive feel for customer relations had landed him a good salary and a brand-new Blackberry, not to mention a chunky car allowance that meant he could afford a nice BMW. Topping it all off was this extremely stylish flat in a converted Victorian house in Clapham. Not bad for a Yorkshire lad of twenty-five whose career at school had been sketchy, to say the least.

The klaxon sounded again. This time he killed the noise and got out of bed and into the bathroom. He looked in the mirror as he shaved and nodded to himself.

Not bad, Foreshaw, not bad. Five nine, eleven stone, a trim body, dark blue eyes. Styled blond hair cut fashionably atop a heart-shaped face. A long, straight nose, which a close friend had once labelled 'heroic' from some chart he'd found on the web. Alan was amused, remembering how he'd been tempted for days to strut around the office, showing off his heroic nose.

It all added up to a package that guys seemed to find attractive, to judge by some of the looks he got when he was out on the scene with his friends. It hadn't got him laid recently – in fact he'd not been in the mood lately, certainly not for a one-night stand. Since his close friends Tris and Ian had got together, Alan had found himself craving the closeness that a committed relationship brought: the small domestic routines, the companionship and, let's face it, being in love with somebody and having a future together.

Alan sighed. He finished shaving and stepped into the shower, enjoying the sting of the hot water on his skin. That would wake him up properly, and a quick coffee from that new American coffee shop on the way to the station would set him up for the day.

✛

He was on the platform waiting for his train into town when the phone call came through.

"Is that Mr Foreshaw?"

"That's me. Who's calling?"

"This is Mrs Rodgerson. Hilda Rodgerson, lives next door to your aunt."

"Oh, yes, Mrs Rodgerson, I remember. What can I do for you?"

"It's about your aunt, Alan. I'm sorry to be the bearer of bad news but I'm afraid she's had a bad stroke this morning. They've taken her off to the infirmary."

"Oh, Hilda, I am sorry. Thanks very much for letting me know. I'll have to make some arrangements to get up there and see her."

"Don't delay too long, Alan. I don't think she'll last long now."

"Right. Yes, I understand. And thanks for the warning."

He continued to exchange platitudes with his aunt's neighbour while his brain tried to process the news and what it meant. He looked at his watch; if he hurried, he could just about get home, pack a bag and still be on time for his ten o'clock meeting, especially if he cabbed it directly to the client. Leaving there and going straight to King's Cross, he could be at the hospital in Sedgethwaite by mid-afternoon.

✢

With all the rush of packing, getting to his meeting and catching the train north, Alan had not had time to think more about his aunt. She had been his guardian since the age of nine following the death of his parents in a plane crash in the USA whilst on a business trip.

He would never forget the day that he had first met her. This strange woman arrived at his school with his grandmother, with whom he had been staying during his parents' trip. She had seemed familiar and yet not so, reminding him of his mother but without the softer bits. Auntie Mary seemed angular and rather austere, whereas Mum had been soft and more huggable.

"This is your Auntie Mary, Alan," his gran had said. "And I'm afraid we've got some very sad news for you."

Thus it was that Alan had found himself under his aunt's guardianship in her house in Sedgethwaite, sixty miles from his own home, his school and everything he had known during this short life. He had been totally traumatised.

But her kindness and love had been strong, even if her nature had indeed been rather austere. Her strong beliefs meant that she could not approve of Alan's lifestyle; they had become distant after he had acknowledged his sexuality in the year after he left for London. They had stayed in touch, and she had travelled south several times to see him, but her disapproval loosened the bond between them. And now she was going, leaving Alan completely and utterly alone in the world.

His earlier dark mood returned. He stared gloomily out of the window as the train pulled into Leeds. It was raining. Typical.

✛

As soon as he arrived in Sedgethwaite, Alan went straight to the hospital to find out how his aunt was. The news was not good: she was hanging on, still fighting to the last, but the doctor was honest almost to the point of brutality. Auntie Mary was unlikely to live for more than a few days at the outside, and she probably would not regain consciousness.

Unable to face going to her house for the time being, Alan booked himself into the most upmarket hotel in Sedgethwaite before talking to his boss. After giving him an update, he arranged to take a week's compassionate leave.

He ate an uninspired meal in the hotel's uninspiring

restaurant, and swallowed a couple of glasses of uninspiring wine. The bar was largely empty, so he retreated to his room to catch up one some e-mails and watch some mindless TV to numb himself into sleep.

He was starting to feel drowsy when his phone buzzed with a text; it was his best friend, Tristram, asking where the hell he was and why he hadn't called. Because Tris's partner, Ian, worked with Alan, he had picked up on the sudden need for compassionate leave.

Alan was touched by Tris's evident concern and quickly dialled his number. "Hi, Tris, sorry not to have been in touch. A bit of a shitty day all round."

"So I gather," his friend replied. "Ian said that you took leave and hared off to Yorkshire. Something about your aunt?"

"Yes, she had a stroke this morning. Prognosis not good, I'm afraid."

"Oh, I'm sorry, Alan, that's seriously bad news. I know you were fond of the old girl. Are you at her house?"

"No, I couldn't face that. I booked into a hotel for a couple of nights, just to get my bearings."

"And are you okay? Do you need some company, because I could...'

"No, Tris, don't worry. I'm fine, really. It was just a bit of a shock, that's all. Her neighbour rang me whilst I was waiting for the train this morning. I did my morning meeting and dashed up here on the first train I could get."

"And what did the doctor say exactly?"

"She's unconscious and not expected to wake up again," Alan replied, his mood darkening as he realised the import of his words once more. "They reckon she'll only last a couple of days, if that."

"Crikey, Alan, That's horrid. What are you going to do?"

"I thought I'd stay up here for a while and see what happens. The firm owes me some time off, and it's not too hectic at the moment. I'll have to pluck up the courage to go round to the house as well, especially if this is actually the end for her."

"Look, you must tell us if you need anything – help, advice or just company. Just say the word, dear boy."

"I will, promise. Love to Ian."

"And from him, my dear. He's sitting right here. Now keep in touch. Let me know how things are going."

"Promise."

"I know you. You'll go into your shell and sit there feeling miserable. You mustn't, all right?"

"Message received."

The conversation ended, and Alan was once again on his own. He was touched by the concern in Tris's voice. They'd been close friends for nigh on five years and shared a flat for three of them. They'd seen each other through various emotional crises, then Alan had introduced Tris to Ian, a friend from work. Ian and Tris had promptly fallen for each other in a big way and were now happily settled together. Meanwhile Alan and Tris remained very close, talking on the phone or texting most days.

✥

Alan had Tris met during his first few months in London. He had been very lonely and rather terrified; as an eighteen-year-old who'd only been to the capital once before, he was completely at sea, living in a hostel. He managed to negotiate his way from the hostel to the office every day, but knew virtually nothing about the city or its life.

They met in a pub near Alan's office, to which he'd been taken several times by colleagues from the agency who often went there straight from work for a couple of hours. That night most of his colleagues had already headed off to meet loved ones or go home; Alan was just thinking about doing the same when this guy walked in with a face like thunder, clearly very annoyed. Focused on his anger and the need for a drink, he tripped over a stool and almost fell into Alan's lap, knocking the remains of his drink flying.

Tris was horrified. "Oh, I say. Look, I'm terribly sorry. Are you okay? Let me buy you another drink. What was it?"

"Thanks, but it's fine. I was just leaving anyway."

"No, I insist," Tris replied anxiously. "It was entirely my fault. I've just been stood up and I was so cross I wasn't paying attention."

Alan reluctantly agreed to the drink, captivated by this charming stranger with his brown hair, sharp cheekbones and regular features. His evident pleasure when Alan agreed to accept the drink was infectious, and his bright blue eyes sparkled.

Within ten minutes, Tris had invited Alan to dinner instead of the boyfriend who'd stood him up. By the end of the evening, they'd become firm friends. Within a month, they were flatmates in a very elegant apartment in Kensington where Tris lived, funded by his parents.

At the time Alan could not have said why they'd clicked so well: they were from totally different social backgrounds and had sharply contrasting attitudes. They were both gay but somehow that did not come into the equation, since they were always friends rather than lovers.

Alan had wondered about this many times over the years: why had they become so close? Tris was a public schoolboy with a First from Oxford and plans to study law; what had he seen in a naïve, gauche nineteen-year-old office boy from industrial West Yorkshire?

Whatever it was that had brought them together had lasted, and their friendship deepened over the years. During that time Tris introduced Alan to a whole new world culturally and socially, broadening his horizons in all sorts of ways. It was the confidence that Tris had instilled in him, alongside his own natural intelligence and ambition, that had given Alan the success he had achieved so far. It was a precious gift.

✛

Warmed by Tris's concern, Alan succeeded in going to sleep but his rest was fitful in an overly-hot room with no opening windows. He awoke feeling unsettled and fidgety; he decided to go into Leeds during the morning for a look around before returning to the hospital for afternoon visiting.

He took the bus and enjoyed the sights, wallowing in nostalgia for his teenage years. Once in the city centre, he looked for the particular shops that had so been important to David and him on their regular Saturday afternoon visits.

He could still remember the route they had taken, looping round the city centre in a circle from the bus station. If they could afford it, a burger and a milkshake from a stall in the market had been part of the routine.

Clothes and records had been the main attractions in those days. Though he still collected CDs to some extent, Alan's tastes had changed from the mid-1980s' pop that had been the staple of the singles collections that he and David built up during their teenage years. Walking up The Headrow, he realised that he didn't even know where his collection of vinyl, cassettes and CD singles was – at Auntie Mary's house, he presumed.

He whiled away a couple of hours in the city centre, spending too much on some new clothes to cheer himself up, then headed back to the bus station for the return trip to Sedgethwaite. As he took in his surroundings he realised that they very different from what they'd been used to on their Saturday afternoon jaunts. A steel-and-glass waiting area had replaced the ancient 1930s' shelters he and David had been used to. He remembered that the terminal had been rebuilt a few years earlier, reopening with a big fanfare just before he left to go to London. It was functional rather than elegant, but was generally well maintained. The concourse smelt of cooked food – a mixture of Cornish pasties and stale bacon – with a background of the diesel fumes wafted into the building on the breeze from the stands outside.

It was certainly busy, with a long row of stands serving the suburbs as well as more distant places such as Harrogate, Skipton and Scarborough. Electronic displays directed him to the stand for the Sedgethwaite bus, and he pushed his way steadily through the milling crowds – mainly pensioners and teenagers, he noticed – to find the correct place.

As he approached, he noticed that a bus was already there with its doors open. A queue of people snaked back onto the concourse as passengers waited to pay their fare or show their passes to the driver. Alan joined the queue and watched as it edged forward. He would be glad to get on board; the carrier bags were heavy and starting to cut into his hands.

As he moved towards the doors, he suddenly remembered that he would need to show his return ticket. He began to manoeuvre his shopping in order to find it, feeling in his pockets and eventually remembering that it was in his wallet. The woman behind him sighed heavily at the delay, and he shot her an apologetic glance. Ticket in hand, he boarded the bus and lifted his ticket for inspection. Only then did he look up and make eye contact with the driver for his trip.

It was David Edgeley.

Veering off Course

Chapter 3

David

The day got off on the wrong foot. David overslept, cut himself shaving, and then almost missed the staff bus. He dismissed Pat's bawdy remarks with a grunt. When they arrived at the depot, Jack Davis was in a foul mood as well. Two drivers had failed to report, and they were short of vehicles for the morning rush hour. Consequently, David worked through from six-thirty until ten o'clock with the bus in front not running.

By seven-thirty, it was pouring with rain. As a result, those people that David did manage to pick up were soaked through and fed up. A row was inevitable.

It happened on the 0932 journey into Leeds. David stopped at Skelthorpe Lane and a middle-aged woman boarded. "About bloody time too! Where've you been? Sat on your backside in the canteen, I suppose."

David gritted his teeth. "No, love. There's one off in front, I'm afraid."

"One? More like bloody six, the time I've been waiting. You lot want a bomb behind you!"

David ignored this. "Where are you wanting, love?"

The woman appealed to her fellow passengers. "Hear that? Bloody typical, isn't it? You wait three-quarters of an hour and then they're trying to rush you!"

"Look, love, I'm running late. I've been on duty since half-six and I haven't had a minute to missen. I'm sorry you've had to wait, but it's not my fault."

"Well, if it's not your fault, I'd like to know whose it is. It's about time you lot were nationalised again. Making profits out of us with a rotten service – you should be ashamed!"

"We were nationalised twenty years ago – that's half the bloody trouble!"

"Don't you swear at me, young man!"

David's control finally snapped. "Oh, for God's sake! Are you going to pay your fare or get off?"

The woman drew herself to her full height and took breath to launch another broadside. But a voice from the back of the bus came to David's rescue. "For Christ's sake, woman, sit down! We haven't got all day."

Floored by this, she banged her fare down on the tray and sat down, starting a loud conversation with the woman next to her about rude bus drivers. David was shaking with anger; he drove rather badly into Leeds.

The onslaught resumed in Leeds Bus Station but David had calmed down sufficiently to cope. He packed the still-irate passenger off to see the bus station inspector and went for a cup of tea.

When he got back to his bus, the inspector was waiting for him. Len Hedges was an old-fashioned busman who had worked with David's uncle. He had a wry sense of humour and a permanent twinkle in his eye. "Now then, David lad. What's this about you upsetting sweet old ladies?"

"Come off it, Len. You know me better than that. Besides, she's neither particularly old nor very sweet!"

"She says you swore at her."

"I said 'bloody' once. Nowt else. And besides, she was holding the whole bus up!"

Len grinned. "Mrs Grimshaw is an old acquaintance of mine. She's complained to me about more drivers than you've had hot dinners. But I expect better of you, lad. Don't let 'em get you down!"

"I know, but after a morning like this the last thing I needed was that battle-axe."

"I know how you feel, but it's part of what we do. Now watch it – I've got my eye on you for inspector next time round, and I don't want you buggering it up. Understood?"

David grinned. "All right."

"Now get on with the job."

Len pottered off across the station, pausing to direct some passengers to the correct stand for their bus. David mentally hugged himself, savouring the thought of becoming an inspector. He liked the idea and immediately felt better than he had done all day.

He boarded his bus and quickly loaded the passengers waiting for the 1132 trip to Sedgethwaite. He started his engine and dealt with the waiting queue. Virtually the last person to board was a well-dressed man, about five foot nine with curly blond hair. He'd obviously had trouble finding his ticket, because the woman behind him was looking discontented at the slight delay. He reached the bus and boarded, struggling with a fistful of bulging carrier bags. He had managed to find his ticket, though, and immediately looked up. He smiled broadly.

David recognised him immediately. "Alan Foreshaw!"

Chapter 4

Alan

"Hello, Davy. God, do they let you drive these things now?"

"Cheeky devil! I've been driving for four years come August!"

"That's funny. Auntie Mary didn't mention it – she's kept me up to date with most of t'gossip."

David chuckled. "Just because you live in the big city now, there's no need to mock the accent."

"Sorry – I'd forgotten what it sounds like, that's all. It's six years, you know."

"Aye. Time flies. What brings you back now?"

"Auntie Mary – she's had a stroke."

"I'm sorry to hear that, Al."

Suddenly, Alan caught sight of a man in uniform marching towards this bus, looking at his watch. "Er, Davy – I think that guy wants a word with you."

"Christ! I must get going. I'll see you at the other end. This my last trip, so we can have a chat after I've booked off."

"Great."

✛

Alan sat on the bus and stared out of the window.

David Edgeley, of all people. What the hell happens now?

His mind went back to those first few crucial days at his new junior school. The only thing that had made the days bearable, and eventually forced him out of his shell, had been the kindness of one little boy.

When he'd arrived in Sedgethwaite, Alan was frightened, suspicious and still traumatised by the sudden loss of his parents and everything he knew. He did not want to talk to anybody. But a little boy in his class called David Edgeley had different ideas.

Finding him alone in the playground on his first day at Leeds Road Juniors, David approached him. "Why are you looking sad?" he asked, adding "It's a shame to be sad all the time."

Alan's eyes immediately filled with tears, and he turned his head away from David to hide his distress. He raised his fists to wipe his eyes. Suddenly, he felt somebody's hand on his upper arm, rubbing gently. It was David. He kept up the motion for a couple of minutes until Alan calmed himself again.

Little did David know that, in that short time and with that simple gesture, he had established a lifelong bond. The bell rang shortly afterwards, signalling the end of afternoon break. They broke their contact and headed back inside.

At morning break the next day, Alan once again headed for a corner of the playground away from everybody else. After a few moments, David joined him. "Hope you're feeling better today," he said quietly. "You're still looking sad. Feel like talking yet?"

Alan thought for a moment but shook his head. David looked at him kindly, his eyes full of concern. "Okay. When you're ready. I think it'd help, though. When you're feeling bad, telling somebody always helps."

Alan nodded and the ghost of a smile passed his lips. The bell rang and it was time to go in.

At the lunch break, after much hesitation, Alan found the words to explain. Telling the story brought back his tears. David held his hand for a few minutes – and that made Alan feel a whole lot better.

The next day at morning break David asked another question: "Would you like to be my friend?" He spoke in a small, solemn voice. "I thought it might cheer you up a bit if I asked," he added. "You know, about being friends."

Alan nodded vigorously and smiled. 'Thanks. I'd like that."

And that was how it had all begun, sixteen long years ago. They'd been good times. He and Davy had got up to all sorts of mischief together – and landed in quite a lot of trouble at times – but his overwhelming memory of those years was of constant laughter. At themselves, at their teachers, at their parents. Everything had seemed to be a huge joke.

Until it wasn't any more. By his early teens Alan had realised that he was attracted to other boys, and one in particular. Until the revelation of that last night before he left for London, he had assumed that wouldn't play well, even with his best pal. He needed to get away from his adopted town. He began applying for jobs and eventually got the post as a junior in the advertising agency where he now worked.

✛

As they pulled into Sedgethwaite Bus Station, Alan woke from his reverie. Here he was, six years on, back in what had become his home town, faced with the same young man that he had run away from. And, he was horrified to realise, feeling exactly the same way about him.

Once David had completed his signing-off procedures at the end of his shift, the two of them headed to a coffee shop across the square from the bus station. The mechanics of getting the drinks allowed David to adjust his thoughts. Six years had certainly made a difference: Alan looked sleek and handsome in his well-cut, expensive clothes, very different from David's dowdy bus-driver's uniform. Moving down south had obviously been a success.

"How's London then?" he asked.

"Great, thanks. I'm in advertising now – making far too much money, and thoroughly enjoying life. And you?"

David concentrated on stirring his tea for a moment before replying. "I – um – married Mona, you know."

"Yes, I remember," Alan murmured, recalling his disappointment and sadness when he'd received the wedding invitation.

"We've two boys, Tommy who's five, and Kevin, three. We got a council house on Beckett's Hill, but we're going to buy somewhere in the autumn."

Alan detected a note of pride in David's voice but at the same time there was something slightly off about the way he said the words, as if he were trying too hard. He refrained from comment and the conversation moved on.

"That's good. How's Mona?"

"Fine. She'd like to see you, I'm sure."

"I don't think so, somehow," Alan responded. "She never really approved of me, you know."

David laughed. "No, you're right there, lad. A disruptive influence, she called you."

Alan finished his tea. "Look, I must get off to the hospital – it'll be visiting time soon, and I need to know what's going on. I'll be at a loose end this evening. Do you fancy a pint, for old times' sake?"

David hesitated but then smiled. "Aye, why not? I haven't been out for ages, and it's my rest day tomorrow."

"Right, you're on. I'll see you in the Boot and Shoe around nine."

"Great. I'll be there."

Veering off Course

Chapter 5

David

Mona was baking when David got home. "You're late," she said. "Get held up?"

"I met Alan Foreshaw – from school, you remember? He's come back up because his Auntie Mary's had a stroke."

"Yes, I remember Alan. Pity it took a stroke for him to come and see his auntie. He never did when she were well."

"He said she didn't want him to."

Mona snorted.

"Anyway, it was nice to see him again."

"Happen," replied his wife noncommittally.

"He's asked me to go for a pint tonight."

"Tonight? A shame you couldn't go, then."

"Why not?"

"You didn't say yes, did you?"

"Shouldn't I have?"

"Oh, David. You know damned well Mum and Dad are coming for tea."

"Oh hell, aye! I forgot all about that. Still, I'm not seeing Alan till nine."

Mona threw the rolling pin down in exasperation. "But we specially fixed it for tonight because you're off tomorrow!"

"They're coming to see you and the boys, not me. They won't mind."

"Maybe not, but I do. It looks rude."

"Look, I haven't seen Alan for nigh on six years. I see your parents every bloody week!"

"That's not the point."

"And anyway, last night you were moaning because I never go out. Now you're moaning 'cos I am doing!"

"I suppose if you're determined to go, I might as well shut up, but—"

"Yes, do that! I'm going upstairs for a wash and a lie down." David turned away angrily.

"What about your dinner?"

"Stick it in a pan. I'll eat it later."

"But it's your favourite – meat and potato pie."

"I said I'll eat it later! Now leave me alone."

He stormed out of the kitchen, almost knocking little Kevin for six. Mona fought back her tears, but Kevin did not and started to wail. One of the pies burned, so David's dinner went into the dustbin after all.

✣

Mona's mother, Cheryl, was a disappointed woman – and not only because her son-in-law was rude enough to go out on a night when she and her husband were visiting.

She still thought of herself as attractive, and she took a great deal of trouble over her appearance. Her shoulder-length, honey-blonde hair was a tribute to her colourist's art. The hair framed a high-domed forehead and a longish straight nose. Her rather disagreeable nature was signalled by her lips: they were thin and prone to disappear almost completely when she was cross, which happened quite often. They also had a semi-permanent downward twist, possibly because of her frequent sense of irritation.

As a terrific snob and a social climber, she had been horrified when her Mona had upped and married a bus driver and gone to live in a council house. That was very far from the dream she had conceived for her daughter when Mona was growing up in the 1980s; Cheryl had imagined that Mona would marry a nice-looking bank manager or lawyer, and live in an 'executive home' with the obligatory two point four children while hubby drove the firm's Cortina.

Cheryl spoke with a mock-refined accent, rather reminiscent of a 1950s' elocution lesson, unlike her husband Brian who had a strong Yorkshire accent that he frequently exaggerated in order to irritate his wife.

Brian was a kind man who always reminded David of the ineffectual prison officer in the television comedy *Porridge*. He was well-meaning and liberal, and saw the best in everybody; he would give a stranger the shirt off his back if it would help them. Of medium height, with a round, gentle face and a slight stoop, he had very poor eyesight and wore glasses with thick pebble lenses that gave him a look of perpetual anxiety.

Mind you, David thought as they sat round the dining

table having tea, being married to Cheryl gave him a lot to be anxious about. Nevertheless, David was fond of his father-in-law, not only because of his gentle demeanour and generosity of spirit but also because he felt so sorry for him. Who wouldn't be anxious if they had to put up with a snobbish, disagreeable and profoundly boring wife?

Normally David managed to tune out his mother-in-law but she had a new topic of conversation today that got under his skin. She had found God. More precisely, she had found Myrtle Jenkins, a new friend who would, she believed, help her to ascend the social ladder by another few rungs.

Consequently, the first half-hour of the meal with Mona's parents was taken up by a detailed description of Myrtle's virtues, house, magnificent taste in clothes and enhanced social status – which entailed her attending several annual events frequented by the great and the good of Sedgethwaite, including the mayoral banquet, charity balls and gala concerts. With a pointed look at Brian, Cheryl lamented the lack of such highlights in her own life.

Cheryl drew their attention to the Church of England in general and the affairs of All Saints, Dewsbury Road in particular whilst Moira served pudding ('dessert' as Cheryl insisted on calling it). Myrtle attended All Saints, an evangelical establishment widely known throughout the area as being anti-permissive in general, and anti-gay in particular. The vicar was one Reverend Archibald Hillier. David had heard of him – in fact there could have been few people in Sedgethwaite who hadn't. He was very charismatic, with a penchant for publicity; he was a regular blogger, and had acquired a regular spot on local radio as well as a column in the local paper.

Cheryl was clearly very taken with the Rev Archie, as he was known. She had quickly become a member of his church and his 'fan club', a large group of women of a certain age who hovered about him, hanging on his every word and catering for his every material need.

"And of course he's against all these homosexuals infecting our society and preying on our young people."

"Oh, quite right, Mother," said Mona. "They should be locked up."

David shifted uneasily in his seat and looked up, catching his father-in-law's glance. He lifted his eyes heavenwards.

"Now, you two, don't be so nasty. People like that can't help it," Brian told his wife and daughter.

"What do you know?" Cheryl virtually spat the words at her husband. "The Rev Archie says they choose to turn away from God and into the ways of sin," she continued in her prim little voice, which was getting on David's nerves even more than usual. "He says they'll all go to hell in a handcart."

"'Let he who is without sin cast the first stone'," quoted Mona's father.

"That's my view as well," said David. "We shouldn't judge other people and their lives by who they sleep with."

"Oh well, really!" Cheryl interjected, wriggling with indignation. "Was there any need to bring *bed* into it?"

"But you started it, Mother," Mona pointed out. "Mentioning gay people."

"Such a stupid euphemism!" Cheryl replied. "Why can't we simply call them perverts and have done with it?"

David glared at his mother-in-law and rose from the table. "I'll thank you not to use such language in our house, especially in front of the boys."

Cheryl tightened her mouth with irritation, once again prompting her lips to disappear almost completely.

"And by the way," David added, getting up from the table, "I'm going out for a drink with a very old friend of mine. Please excuse me, but he's only here for a few days and I haven't seen him for six years. I'll bid you goodnight." He left the room.

The last sound he heard was his mother-in-law's indignant voice exclaiming, "Well, really!"

Chapter 6

Alan

Alan was already in the Boot and Shoe when David arrived shortly after nine. "Hi! What'll you have?"

David hesitated; he noticed a glass of what looked like wine at the table where Alan was sitting – but surely not, not in a Yorkshire pub!

Alan followed David's line of sight. "Oh, don't worry about the white wine – it's part of my keep-fit thing. It's the only alcohol I'm allowed! Now, what's it to be? A pint of best?"

"Aye, go on then."

"I don't think they're used to men drinking wine here," said Alan, returning to their table.

David grinned. "Shouldn't think it happens very often round here, any road – leastways except in the Dog in town," he replied.

"Why the Dog?"

"Sedgethwaite's gay pub."

"My, we have advanced in the last six years," Alan joked. "A gay pub here? In Sedgethwaite? Wow. What's it like?"

"Er – I'm hardly in a position to know," retorted David, looking at Alan with a slightly pained expression.

"Oh, I'm sorry, I didn't mean…"

"Don't be daft, lad," replied David, joining in the laughter. "How's Auntie Mary, then?"

Alan sighed. "Not too good, I'm afraid. She hasn't recovered consciousness, and they don't think she will. It's probably the best way. She was still a lively old stick, and being paralysed or unable to speak would drive her up the wall."

"Aye. A shame though. When I think… I used to be terrified of her when we were kids. Do you remember the first time you asked me back for tea?"

"God! Yes. It must have been when we were at Leeds Road Juniors…"

✛

Any initial awkwardness was swept away quickly by a wave of reminiscence and a steady flow of alcohol. Thus it was that, by eleven o'clock, Alan had polished off a whole month's allowance of dry white wine, whilst David owned up to drinking more beer in two hours than in the previous year.

However, neither of them was uproariously drunk; indeed, Alan was surprised at how sober he felt. They left the pub slightly before time was called and walked towards the town centre.

"Well, Davy, lad," said Alan in a broad Yorkshire accent, "it's been a reet good neet. I've had a smashing time."

"Me too – just like the old days." He sighed. "Are you

truly happy, then, down there?"

Alan laughed. "Yes, old son, I am. I know you find it difficult to believe in life outside Sedgethwaite, but it does exist. I've got a good job, a great flat and a BMW. It's a nice life. I've got no complaints." He paused to think for a moment. "No. No complaints."

"I did wonder sometimes," said David.

"Yes, I bet you did. And what about you? Are you truly happy?"

As had happened that morning in the cafe, David looked uncomfortable. When he spoke, he was clearly on the defensive. "The kids are great and Mona's fine. She's a good cook and a good housekeeper. I think I said we're buying a house in the autumn, and they told me today I could be line for inspector next time round. No, I can't complain."

They walked on in silence for a moment, before Alan spoke. "Answer the question, Davy."

"I have, haven't I?"

"Davy, even after six years I know you too well to let you get away with that. And please, whatever you do, don't try to deceive yourself. That's the dusty road to death. Now, I'll ask you again. What about you? Are you truly happy?"

"No. I'm bored, fed up, sick of the job, sick of being married and altogether fucking miserable. There, does that make you feel better?"

"No, but at least it's the truth."

"And perhaps you could kindly tell me what bloody good it does to say it out loud."

They had reached the entrance to Alan's hotel. "I've got one of those little kettles in my room. Come up and have a cup of coffee."

"I ought to get home. Mona'll be worried."

"Oh, come on. Ten minutes won't make much difference." Alan grinned suddenly. "Besides, if I've upset your peace of mind that much, the least I can do is try to restore it."

"All right. But no more than ten minutes, mind."

Alan noticed that David had obviously never been inside a large hotel before. His friend was looking round all the time, curious about the interior and fascinated by the mechanics of a key system based on a plastic card. Alan watched with amusement as David explored the tiny bathroom and the bedroom, eyes wide and muttering to himself.

"Bloody clever design, these rooms."

"Yes, I suppose they are. I'd never thought about it before. Now, do you want coffee or another drink? There'll be stuff in the minibar."

"Oh, just coffee, thanks. Otherwise I really will be pissed."

Alan busied himself with the small kettle and the sachets of coffee, milk and sugar. David took his jacket off, then slipped off his shoes and stretched himself out on the bed. He looked over at Alan and beamed at him. "This is the life, eh, lad?"

Alan put the coffee cups down on the bedside table and sat on the edge of the bed next to David.

"I'm a bit drunker than I thought," David giggled. "But not so drunk as to miss your tricks. You can't have been telling the truth just now about being happy. You can't be, 'cos you didn't mention any one special like a partner or girlfriend. Nobody's happy when they're lonely."

"Actually, I think that's highly debatable, but no matter. I didn't mention that side of my life because I wasn't sure how you'd react. How much do you remember about that last night before I went to London?"

"Enough to know what you're trying to say." David sat up and swung his legs onto the floor, moving next to Alan, so that their legs were touching from hip to ankle bone. He paused and sipped his coffee. Then he looked Alan directly in the eye and spoke in a low voice. "To tell the truth, I remember every single detail of that night. Hardly a day has gone by when I haven't thought of you and what happened. There, is that what you wanted to know?"

Alan watched, horrified, as David's eyes filled with tears and he looked away. "Christ, Davy. I'm sorry."

"Whatever for?"

Alan shrugged. "Everything really. Kissing you that night, running off to London and now coming back today. Each time I've knocked you off your perch and left you floundering in the dark, haven't I?"

David shook his head. "Not your fault. It's my life I'm busy fucking up – oh and Mona's, I suppose. Did you know?"

"I didn't – at least not until the moment I saw you this morning." Gently, Alan reached out and lifted David's chin. He kissed him.

After a moment's hesitation, David responded. The kiss was sweet and gentle. It was like coming home.

Now I know what I've been missing for the last six years.

Alan moaned into David's mouth and moved to hold him in a full embrace. David responded, rolling on top of Alan, who immediately wrapped his legs round his friend's waist.

Suddenly David stopped. Alan opened his eyes, puzzled. He watched as the expression on David's face went from passionate to terrified, as if a switch had been thrown. Eyes wide open, but with fear rather than curiosity this time, David quickly disentangled himself from the embrace and got up from the bed. Alan looked up at him, wondering what on earth had just happened.

David stood for a moment, straightening his clothing, head downcast, unable to meet Alan's eyes. Then he spoke. "Sorry, Al," he said, quietly. "I can't do this. Got to go."

He turned and left the room without looking back, shutting the door quietly.

✛

Alan remained where he was for a few moments, staring at the ceiling and tracing the course of a hairline crack in the plaster. A stray tear found its way from the corner of his eye and dropped on to the bedding, followed by another, then another.

He roused himself quickly. When he'd arranged to see David tonight, he'd speculated idly about whether something like this would happen but had been determined that it wouldn't. After all, there could be no future for any form of relationship between them even if they wanted one. Apart from family complications, they lived two hundred miles apart. And those two hundred miles might as well have been two million, because their lives had diverged six years earlier and the gap had grown ever wider.

No, they had simply been impelled by nostalgia for a friendship long over. Alan had been feeling vulnerable tonight because of his aunt's illness and the memories unlocked by returning to Sedgethwaite. In any case, he'd been feeling lonely after moving out of Tris's place. That was his excuse for what had happened. And he could certainly not blame David for leaving now. It had been the right thing to do.

His mind continued in this vein as he moved round the room, tidying the coffee cups and getting ready for bed. It was only when he lay down again that he remembered how David had felt in his arms for those few minutes. He closed his eyes and hugged the memory close. It had felt exactly the same as that night six years earlier: they fitted together perfectly.

David was his soulmate; he had been since that day in the playground sixteen years earlier. The boy who had rubbed his shoulder to make him feel better held the missing pieces of Alan's life. Alan only felt whole when he was in his old friend's company.

Another stray tear trickled down his face as he realised that he would have to reconcile himself to never feeling whole again.

Veering off Course

Chapter 7

David

David did not start to react to what had happened until he was halfway home. It was late, very late – after one, in fact – but the last bus had gone and he hadn't got enough cash on him for a taxi, so he had no option but to walk.

It was okay actually, because it was a clear night and maybe the exercise would do him good. He hoped it would help to clear his mind, which at the moment was a jumble of disconnected thoughts. A big part of him regretted bailing out on Alan. Holding and being held by his lifelong friend had felt right, as if he'd come home. Exactly as it had the last time, all those years ago,

But he wasn't a horny, confused teenager any more; he was a married man with two children, and he had responsibilities towards them. He had to focus on that fact. It was all very well for Alan; he was a single man with a life in London, where the gay stuff was much more normal. This was industrial West Yorkshire, for Christ's sake. Real men didn't screw each other – and he was a real man, wasn't he? He'd spent the last six years proving it, after all.

But somehow his own words did not ring true. David knew in his heart of hearts that, if he'd had the courage, he would have followed Alan to London six years earlier and been with him all this time. The pattern of his life would now be so different. Above all, he would have been spared the depressing process of rebuffing his wife's amorous advances until he couldn't avoid some form of response, and then straining every nerve to try to ensure that he completed the job. Compare that with the arousal he had felt with Alan tonight... Still, at least he now had another memory that he could use to fantasise when he had to.

He sighed. What the hell was he going to do now? Maybe he didn't need to worry. Alan would be gone in a couple of days, back to London. When his aunt died, he'd never have cause to come back here. And that would be that. David would be able to forget him.

But even as that thought entered his mind, he knew it was untrue. Whatever happened, he would never forget Alan Foreshaw.

✛

David stayed in bed until after ten the next morning. That was not unusual on his rest day, especially after a week of early turns. He rarely slept long, though, what with Mona getting young Tommy off to school and little Kevin charging about the place. This morning was no exception, despite his late arrival home.

All the guilt and fear that David had expected to feel the previous night was now pressing in on him. His reactions were exactly as he remembered them from that February morning six years earlier: belief that what had nearly happened was evil and unnatural; self-disgust that he had allowed things to go as far as they had, and fear that such behaviour would alienate him from his way of life and his family.

And yet... Another voice within him spoke a different message: that last night could have been so much more; that the way he'd felt was more than a one-off aberration but was a manifestation of a part of his nature that he had tried to bury. A hurried marriage to Mona and the swift production of children had succeeded for a while, but they offered only a temporary refuge from his own nature. Having sex with Alan six years ago had been one of the best experiences of his life; last night could have been the same if he'd allowed it to be. Most frightening of all was the fact he wanted it to happen again – and soon.

In fact, if Alan walked through that door now...

His rising excitement was brought to an abrupt end by Mona's voice. "Are you getting up this side of Christmas?"

Oh dear. She did not sound happy.

"Yes, love. Just coming." He smirked at his own unintended pun. He got out of bed, and caught sight of himself in the wardrobe mirror. His voices resumed their conflict. One tried to make him feel ashamed of his body, telling him that it had been cruelly violated by Alan. The other answered that this was the body, the body that Alan had once said was beautiful and which had, with Alan, given David the only true sexual satisfaction he'd ever known.

Again, Mona's voice broke into his reverie. "If you're

having a bath, put the immersion on, will you?"

"Right, love."

But what now? What the bloody hell am I going to do about it all?

"David, are you up yet?"

He glanced down at himself, and smirked at his reflection in the mirror. "And how!"

✛

"God, I thought you were going to be in that bath all day! What have you been doing?"

"I wasn't that long! Its only half-ten."

"But you're holding me up. I suppose you want some breakfast now."

David ignored this and began a dialogue with himself. "Good morning, my love. I trust you slept well? Isn't it a lovely day? Yes, isn't it? I slept beautifully, thank you."

Mona smiled despite herself. "All right, I'm sorry. But coming in at nearly two in the morning, waking the whole street... I was worried to death. Wherever had you been?"

"Talking. To Alan," he replied.

"Oh, sure. And I was born yesterday. Why don't you tell me the truth? He took you to some club or other, didn't he?"

"No, he didn't! We stayed in the Boot and Shoe till just before closing and then walked back to his hotel – he's staying at the new one near the Market. Quite posh, you know. And we talked. I missed the last bus, so I had to walk home."

"David Edgeley, you're the biggest liar on God's earth!

Whatever would you talk about until gone one in the morning?"

"All sorts of things – life, what we did when we were kids, that sort of stuff."

"Well, I never did. First, you upset my mum and dad by choosing to go out on the one day in the week when they come to see us, then you stay out until God knows what time in the morning. And you come down here the next day expecting me to believe that you were talking all night."

"What do you think I was doing?"

"I told you! I think Alan Foreshaw took you off to a club and got you off with some woman. I know his influence of old – he'd do anything to do me down!"

David started to laugh; he knew that it was the wrong thing to do, but he couldn't help it. The whole scene was so bizarre, especially in view of what had actually occurred.

"You might think it's funny but I don't. I slave here night and day, keeping you and the kids and trying to run a nice home. And all you can do is throw it back in my face and laugh at me." Tears started.

David reached out to her. "Mona, love, don't cry. You've got yourself all worked up about summat and nowt. Once and for all, I did *not* go to a club with Alan last night. We stayed in the pub and then went back to the hotel. I did *not* go with any woman last night. Understood?"

Mona turned to face him. The venom in her voice as she spoke took him aback. "You're a liar, David. Something happened last night. I know I'm right, and you won't convince me otherwise, even if you stand there and tell lies until you're blue in the face."

David's face fell. How did she know? How could she?

"You see! It's in your face! Get used to this, my lad! You don't get any food cooked in this house until you tell me the truth. If you want any breakfast, you'd better go to the bus station canteen!"

"All right! If that's how you want it, I'll go." David got up and went towards the hall. "But if you can't trust me enough to believe me when I'm telling the truth, then it's a bloody poor do, that's all I can say."

"If so, you'd better stop talking in your sleep!"

The front door slammed as David left the house but he had heard her parting shot, and it made his stomach turn over.

✥

The bus station canteen was crowded when David arrived. It was getting on for lunchtime, and it usually got quite busy as early- and late-turn staff overlapped. A gang of the lads crowded round the notice-board, laughing and joking.

"Hallo, Pete. What's up?" David asked.

"Hello, David. I thought you were on a rest day."

"I am, but I'm in the doghouse with the wife, so I came out to get some peace and a bit of breakfast."

"Oh, dear. Like that, is it?"

"Aye. What's all the fuss about, then?"

"Oh, it's the coaching lot. Apparently, we're getting some work on a new London service this summer. They're looking for volunteers to drive on it."

"Oh. You interested?"

"Not me, lad. Too much like hard work, driving up and down the bloody Ml all day and every day. Besides, the wife'd never stand for the overnights."

"Overnights?" asked David.

"Aye. There's a London sleep-out duty every night, apparently. Anyway, must dash – I've got the 1230 to Huddersfield. See thee."

"Aye, tarra, Pete."

David ordered his breakfast and sat down, reflecting that it was somehow inevitable that the subject of a London service should crop up today.

"Hello, young man. Sworn at any little old ladies lately?"

"Me? What?" He looked up to see Len Hedges. "Oh, it's you! Hello, Len. Sorry, I was miles away."

"And what's your excuse for being here on your rest day? Mine is that I had to come into town for some shopping."

"I'm in the doghouse. A night on the tiles, I'm afraid."

"Oh dear. Bad, is she?"

"She'll come round."

"Good. Now, I'm glad I've seen you. What about this London service?"

"What do you mean?"

"Are you going to apply?"

"I hadn't thought of doing." The alarm bells were sounding inside him. Surely, this was being sent to tempt him. Regular overnight stays in London? What would that do for his resolve?

"I think you should. It would be bloody good experience for you, David lad. Think of it: you'll have done the lot – buses, coaches, local, motorway, London. You'll be well-qualified for the future. Mind you," Len finished with a laugh, "you'd have to make sure Mona didn't think you were going for the night life."

"Oh, bloody hell, no. Anyway, they tell me you can't afford the beer in London."

"You're right, there. The wife's nephew told me that it's nigh on fifty pence a pint dearer down there in some pubs."

"Bloody hell! Well, that proves it, doesn't it? I wouldn't be applying for the sake of the boozy nights!"

"Aye, you're right there. But seriously, think on, lad. There's nowt like all-round experience to fit you for future promotion."

"Great, Len, thanks. I will think about it seriously."

He could not help but chuckle. Regular trips to London, overnight stays, possibly regular visits to Alan... It was enough to defeat the strongest resolution.

He set off for the depot and immediately put his name forward.

✛

David's application for the London service was well received and he left there feeling more cheerful than he had done for several weeks. It was quite a pleasant day for March, so he decided to walk at least part of the way home through the park.

On his own for the first time since leaving the house that morning, his mind inevitably returned to the events of the previous night. His reactions were still confused and contradictory.

He could remember every detail of the evening: the

awkward start in the pub; the flood of reminiscence; the walk back to Alan's hotel; going up to the room and lying on the bed; pressing his leg against Alan's, and holding him in his arms...

The memory sent shivers down his spine; surely feelings like that, so warm and exciting, could not be wrong? They were a part of him, weren't they? Part of who he was, which he had been suppressing all his life. He had to own them.

Despite the fact that nothing had happened in the end, last night had been a watershed, a turning point. How could he simply carry on as if nothing had happened? Impossible. And now the London business, cropping up the very next day. That had to be heaven-sent, didn't it? He could meet up with Alan and decide what to do. Thoughts of Alan brought David's mind back to the previous night – his touch, that first kiss...

He emerged from the park at the same moment as the Beckett's Hill bus drew around the corner. He boarded it almost without thinking and was immediately plunged into conversation with George, the driver.

✤

Mona was about to leave the house when David got home. "Oh, hello," she said. "I was going to fetch Tommy."

"I'll come with you if you like."

"That would be nice."

Kevin was in the pushchair, chattering away happily. David and Mona walked in silence. After a few moments, they both started to speak at the same moment. David gave way and let his wife speak first.

"I'm sorry about this morning, love," she said. "I don't know what came over me. It was Alan coming back, I suppose. I always was a bit jealous of you two, and last night brought it all back. You woke me this morning, talking in your sleep about two birds you and Alan had pulled, and taking them back somewhere... I just saw red, I suppose. Especially when it's been so long since you've ... I mean we've ... well, you know."

David did not react for a moment; he was too busy breathing a sigh of relief about what he had said in his sleep. Then he spoke. "I'm glad you're all right now. I couldn't understand what you were on about earlier." He started to chuckle. "But I can tell you what I was talking about in my sleep, because Alan and I had spent most of the evening reminiscing. I'd lay you odds that I was thinking about those two lasses in your class. Do you remember? Tracey and ... um ... Sharon?"

Mona saw the joke too. "Oh, that I do!" she said. "Tracey Merrion and Sharon Morley. God, what a pair! Didn't you and Alan take them to Blackpool one year?"

"We certainly did, and a rum weekend it was, too."

"Oh, well. That explains it, love. I *am* sorry."

"Don't worry. It's over, now," David responded.

By this time, they had reached the school. Young Tommy came charging out to meet his daddy and the family pottered off up the road.

✛

David and Mona spent a pleasant evening in front of the

television. Mona was pleased to notice that he seemed more relaxed than he had for a long time. Obviously, the whole business had cleared the air a bit.

David, meanwhile, was happy to allow the television to divert his thoughts away from The Situation, as he had come to call it. He had not yet raised the London business with Mona; he knew that it had to be done that evening, but he was waiting for the right opportunity. It came as they were washing up the supper things.

"Did you get any news when you were in town?" Mona asked.

"Aye. We're getting some coaches next month, apparently. A new service to London. They're asking for volunteers to drive it."

"Oh, that sounds interesting. Are you going to have a go?"

David breathed another sigh of relief. "I thought I might. But I was a bit worried about the overnights. Would you mind being on your own for a couple of nights a week?"

Mona thought for a moment. "Not really. I mean it's not so very different from when you're on lates, is it? I'm always asleep when you get in from that last Leeds duty."

"True. I hadn't thought of it like that."

"Well, there you are then. Besides, it'll be a change. You've been very restless lately."

"Also true. And Len Hedges seemed to think it would be good experience. He wants me to put in for an inspector's job next time round."

"No! Really? But that's great news! Do you mean to tell me, David Edgeley, that you've sat there all evening knowing all that and not said a word? I don't know."

"I don't like to boast."

"Don't be daft, lad! Now come here and give us a kiss."

✣

When they got to bed a few minutes later, Mona snuggled up to her husband. This time, he relaxed into her embrace and she was not rebuffed. Consequently, Mona went to sleep a good deal happier than she had of late.

David lay awake beside her and listened as her breathing settled into the rhythm of sleep. He suspected that his wife would not have been so pleased if she'd realised that he had only managed to have sex with her tonight by thinking about Alan rather than her. He told himself that trying to compare the two experiences was unfair and impractical, but nevertheless the comparison was made.

He realised just how much he had preferred Alan's company to Mona's. It was true in all sorts of ways: the hardness of his body to the softness of hers; Alan's responsiveness compared to Mona's passivity, and – much to his own surprise – a desire to be a receiver as well as a giver. Goodness, where had that come from? But he knew now that he wanted that, and soon. He needed to feel Alan inside him, to express a decade of affection and friendship with physical love. Another part of him was shocked at his own thoughts.

This process was like the steady closing of a vice as the feelings and emotions that had passed through his mind from time to time all day bore in on him again.

He had a growing conviction that there could be no going back, no more hiding behind a wife, no more pretending that fatherhood was proof of his masculinity, whatever that was. He was, at the very least, bisexual. He was attracted to both men and women, but probably preferred men. The consequences of that would have to be faced in the end.

His conscience flared up again. Even if he was bisexual, there was no reason to act on it. He had made certain vows and promises when he married Mona, and he had a duty to the two children she had borne him. There was no getting away from that. He was not a free agent and to pretend otherwise was idle nonsense.

He shivered uncomfortably, but quickly remembered once more the sensations from the previous night and how it had felt being in Alan's arms. It made him feel warm inside, enabling him to drift off into an uneasy sleep.

Veering off Course

Chapter 8

Alan

Alan was disturbed from a deep sleep by his mobile ringing. He shook himself awake and grabbed the instrument before the call went to voicemail. He did not recognise the number but saw that it was local.

It was the hospital. His aunt had had another stroke and was now in a deeper coma. He should get there as soon as possible.

He rang reception to arrange for a cab, before throwing himself into the shower and into some clothes. He made it into reception in less than ten minutes, at the same moment as the cab pulled up outside.

Once inside the vehicle, he forced himself to calm down. He didn't know why he was rushing; if she was in a coma, it would make no difference to Auntie Mary whether he was there or not. But somehow it was important to him: it mattered that he should be there for her passing, to mark the death of his only living relative.

He grimaced. Truly alone at last.

He had spent most of the previous day at the hospital.

Waking up after his night out with David, he had been unable – or unwilling – to think about what had passed between them, or what it meant for him. He had bustled about, checking e-mails, talking to his boss even though he was supposed to be on leave, and generally keeping his mind occupied.

But the afternoon had been a different prospect. He sat with his aunt for most of the time, holding her hand. He relished the occasional awareness in her eyes or slight squeeze of her hand that meant she knew he was there and appreciated it.

He owed this woman so much. Her special version of tough love had been difficult to cope with at times, especially for a moody teenager. But, despite the fact that she had been brusque and occasionally dismissive of his emotions, she had always made him feel secure and valued. That had meant a lot – it still did – which was one of the reasons he now felt as if his emotions had been through a shredder.

Alan had embraced his sexuality after an initial struggle and was now at peace with it. His aunt had strongly disapproved of that side of his life on religious grounds but had never judged him for it or treated him harshly. They simply did not talk about it.

He told himself that it was ridiculous to feel as raw he did. It was inevitable that he should feel sadness at her imminent passing, but the gut-wrenching loneliness that steadily overtook him as the evening wore on was surely an overreaction. Here he was, a successful young man with a brilliant career ahead of him, a nice flat in London and a wide circle of friends. Why should he feel so lonely?

The inevitable conclusion crashed in on him after a couple of hours sitting there. It was nothing to do with his aunt, but everything to do with Davy. In truth, he had known it all along but had been unwilling to face the fact; it was much easier to file the issue under the heading 'too difficult'.

Bringing out the question again and airing it was not going to solve anything; it was back to this business of feeling whole. For one night six years earlier, and for an even briefer few minutes last night, Alan had known what it was like to feel complete, to be connected to another human being not only physically but through shared experiences, emotions and dreams of the future. The prospect of never feeling like that again, of never holding the only person he had ever truly loved in his arms, was almost more than he could bear.

For the rest of his visit Alan sat at Auntie Mary's bedside, his mood bleak and his eyes wet with unshed tears, cursing the fates that had brought him to this point in his life. Eventually he left the hospital and went back to the hotel. It was well after midnight before he finally fell asleep – and only then because he had consumed too much whisky.

Now, the following morning, as the taxi approached the entrance to Sedgethwaite District Hospital, his mood was little better. The only glimmer of consolation was that, with his aunt's death imminent, he could get out of this godforsaken little town and return to his own life. Maybe then he could start to rebuild it.

He paid the cabbie and set off for the ward. He arrived with a few moments to spare and held his aunt's hand again, but this time only long enough to feel the life force drain away from it.

He stayed long enough to complete the formalities, before leaving the building as quickly as possible. Its particular brand of 1970s' brutalism had not softened over the years, and its appearance was now dilapidated and uncared for as scarce resources were focused on what went on inside. He would be profoundly grateful if he never had to set foot in the place again.

Once outside, he wondered what to do next. The hospital had given him a list of undertakers and he decided to sort out the funeral arrangements. If he could do that today, he could go back to London tonight and only return on the day of the funeral...

But then he remembered that life was not that simple; Sedgethwaite had not finished with him yet. There was Auntie Mary's Will to find and execute, the house to clear and sell, and his own demons to face in going back there – not least his memory of the last night he had spent there as a teenager with David.

He set off towards the town centre with a view to going to the undertakers but could not help feeling that it was a little premature. His poor aunt was barely cold. No, it could wait, at least until after lunch.

He looked up and saw a bus coming along, showing the destination Town Moor. Situated at the northern edge of the built-up area, bordered on one side by the post-war Beckett's Hill housing estate, this huge area of common land rose steeply to a ridge which had spectacular views in two directions: southwards back over the town, or northwards across a broad dale stretching towards the slopes of the northern Pennines.

On a whim, he sprinted to the nearby stop and hailed the bus. He bought a ticket to the terminus. He had a vivid memory of countless walks on the moor with Davy as a boy, chasing butterflies, looking for fantasy elephants, playing hide and seek. He particularly remembered them using the Moor as an alien planet which they explored in a fantasy born of their love of old *Star Trek* episodes. They had hidden for hours from their alien pursuers amongst the limestone outcrops and small copses.

The terminus was near the last of the houses on the estate. Alan left the bus and set off up the hill. The sun was shining now but the wind was still chilly. He wandered aimlessly across the turf for a while, before coming across a path that seemed vaguely familiar.

He followed it to the summit of the ridge and was immediately captivated by the view northwards. He found a limestone outcrop on which to sit and took in the sight that lay before him. It was a beautiful late winter's day; the bright blue sky was criss-crossed by aircraft vapour trails, whilst the sun was bright but quite low in the sky. It flooded the dale below with a subtle, pale golden light; its rays highlighted the bumps and ridges in the fields, and especially the drystone walls that divided them, bringing all the features into sharp relief. Way down in the valley, he caught sight of a little streak of white as one of the season's earliest lambs tried to find its feet.

Alan drank in the view; he had forgotten how spectacular it was. Even in the industrial heartlands of the county it was not all dark satanic mills. Suddenly he had another memory, this time of his aunt bringing him up here not long after the death of his parents. It had been a warm summer's day. This formidable woman, clad in a formal lavender coat that had once been fashionable, with a rather battered toque on her head, had held his hand and pointed out the names of all the distant hills.

"Whenever I wonder about the world and my place in it, Alan lad, I come up here. It refreshes me and reminds me of what a jolly good job God did when He made Yorkshire. Because of that, it renews my faith in Him and all His works, despite all the rotten stuff that happens in the world. Remember, lad, God has a purpose for all of us. If you ever lose sight of yours, come up here and look out over that view."

All these years later, he had no idea what God's purpose was for him, especially as he didn't believe any of that stuff anyway. But his aunt had had faith, and he knew how much it had meant to her. Now she was gone. They'd argued a lot but he would miss her terribly. She'd been the rock in his life; now he felt rootless without her and very, very lonely.

For the first time since he'd felt the life drain from her, he wept for his aunt.

Chapter 9

David

With the morning came more worry, more mind-numbing internal debate. Mona was too busy with household chores to take too much notice of David before lunch, and made it clear that she would rather have him of the way. He decided to try another long walk in the hope that the physical activity would help him sort himself out.

He headed for the moor at the top of their street. Given that he had some time to himself, he could indulge in some "what if?" scenarios.

What if he did decide to come out? Go off to live in London? Suppose he could go and live with Alan? Yeah, sure: nice fantasy, but the fallout would be massive. For a start, what about Mona and the boys? That would mean leaving them and possibly never seeing the boys again. And how could he do that?

He'd have to tell everybody, too: his parents, sisters, work-mates, the bosses, the boys, Mona's mum and dad... They'd all have to be faced, and told ... well, told something, at least.

Yes, he'd have to give some sort of explanation. What other job could he do? Where would he go? How would he maintain Mona and the boys financially? Above all, what could he say to Mona? How could he tell her that he preferred men?

Suddenly, he was almost overwhelmed by fear. It was all very well for Alan; he was used to it by now – being gay was fully a part of his life. Surely what David was now facing only happened to characters in books or TV soaps, not to real people. And certainly not to people like *him*. He was an ordinary bus driver with a family.

He simply did not know what to do.

It was the loneliness that frightened him most. Who could he tell? He had never experienced anything before that he couldn't talk to somebody about. He thought of trying to get in touch with Alan, but Alan wouldn't be bothered now, especially after being left in the lurch the previous night. Anyway, he was too far away, and wouldn't understand what David was going through. After all, Alan had made his decision six years earlier, and without the additional problems of a wife and children.

David left the estate behind him and walked onto the hillside above the town. He was enjoying the sunshine; the view from up here was marvellous and usually he loved it, but this time he was oblivious to it, wrapped in his awful cocoon of fear and dread.

He rounded a bend in the path and saw another figure ahead of him, sitting on an outcrop and looking across the valley. It slowly dawned on him that it was Alan – that he wasn't hundreds of miles away in London but here in Sedgethwaite, dealing with his aunt's final illness. Of course he was.

David walked towards him but Alan did not move.

"Hey. You okay?" David asked.

Surprised by the voice, Alan looked up. His face was a picture of misery and distress. David immediately realised why. "Auntie Mary didn't make it, then?"

Alan shook his head, still unable to speak.

"Oh, Al. I *am* sorry."

At last Alan was able to get some words out, his voice rough with emotion. "Thanks, Davy. You know, I loved her so much and she looked after me for all those years. I never wanted for anything, and she loved me as if I were her own. I shall really miss her."

David sat down on the rock and put his arm across his friend's shoulders. He felt Alan relax into the embrace and let himself go, covering his face with his hands and sobbing quietly. David said nothing, simply held him; he was also remembering the formidable but kind woman who had welcomed him into her home so often over the years.

Eventually Alan calmed down, his emotion spent. He raised his head and looked David in the eye, still sniffling a little. Wiping his eyes with the back of his sleeve, he gave a small, weak smile. "Sorry about that. I know we Yorkshiremen aren't supposed to cry."

"I don't know where that idea came from," David responded, "but it always seemed bloody daft to me."

"Exactly what I was thinking," Alan said, blowing his nose and pulling himself together. "Anyway, what are you doing up here at this time of day?"

"I'm on late turn this week – don't start till three. Mona's cleaning, so I got out of the way. And I needed to think."

"What about, Davy?"

"Us, you daft bugger," he said with gruff affection. "The other night. What happened between us and what it means for the future."

"But nothing did happen, Davy. Surely that's the point."

"I know, I know. I'm sorry. I shouldn't have run out on you. I hope I didn't hurt you too much. I just panicked. Were you totally pissed off with me?"

"No, no. I understood," Alan replied, shaking his head. "Anyway, it was my fault. I shouldn't have let matters get that far."

"Why ever not?"

"Because I'd told myself I mustn't. All day after I met you in Leeds, I kept thinking about my last night here all those years ago ... and about us. What happened, I mean. And I wondered about you, how you'd felt – you know, afterwards."

"Bloody terrified, I can tell you. And so lonely, once you'd gone."

"Is that why you married Mona?"

"Aye. How did you guess?"

"It didn't take much working out, lad. She and I were the only two friends you ever had."

"True. I'd never thought of it like that."

There was a pause, then Alan spoke again. "I'm sorry I didn't come to your wedding, Davy. I just... I couldn't, that's all."

"'S'okay. I understood."

"Anyway, back to the other day. I decided that you'd made your choice by marrying Mona and it wouldn't be fair to barge back into your life and spoil everything. In fact at one stage I decided not to turn up at the pub that night."

"You're kidding! You rotten bugger."

"Shall I tell you why I changed my mind?"

"Aye."

"I remembered your face that morning. You'd seemed so pleased to see me in Leeds. And later, in the café, you were so anxious to tell me how happy you were."

"Is that what you meant the other night when you said you'd expected me to remember your last night here?"

"Spot on. I had a gut feeling that you hadn't actually chosen Mona at all but run away from what happened that night and bumped into her on the way, so to speak."

"Got it in one."

"And now what?"

"God knows, Al. It's all such a mess. I do know that we can't put the clock back, and I mustn't pretend the other night didn't happen like I did before, six years ago. What I do know is that I want you. I want to do what we almost did the other night before I panicked."

Alan turned to look at him, wide-eyed. "Gosh, Davy, that's a lot of decisions for a little fella."

"I know," said David with a smile. "Quite good for a bear of little brain, isn't it?" But his expression grew serious again. "But knowing that doesn't help with sorting out the rest of my life. I don't know where it leaves me and my job, or you, or Mona, or the boys." He paused and gave a short bark of laughter. "You could say that, other than thinking about my dick and what I want to do with it, I haven't made much progress."

"Don't be too hard on yourself, old lad," Alan replied. "It's bloody difficult stuff, all this. And don't forget that doing nothing is still an option."

"How do you mean?"

"I'll be gone in a few days, after Auntie Mary's funeral. You could try to forget it – *us* – and go back to being a good husband and father."

David felt a cold stab of fear. "Is that what you want, then, Al?"

"No, it fucking well isn't, David Edgeley," Alan replied sharply. "I realised the other day how much I've missed you and I don't want to go back to that. But I would, for you if that was what you decided you wanted. Say the word, Davy, and I'll get out of your life for ever."

"Christ, Al. No. You can't! We're only twenty-five, for fuck's sake. I can't spend the next forty or fifty years living a lie, hiding my real self – throwing away a chance of happiness because of a mistake I made six years ago." He paused. "It's just... I know *what* I want to do, but I don't know *how* to do it. I'm frightened, Al. Fucking terrified."

"I know, Davy, I know. I wish I lived nearer."

"I might be able to see you a bit more often in London. We're starting a new contract for an express service next month. It involves an overnight turn and I've applied for one of the jobs."

"Davy, what fantastic news! I do hope you get it. You can come and stay – and I'll show you the sights." Alan waggled his eyebrows, before adding, "*All* of them."

David raised his own eyebrows and smirked at his friend. "That would be great. Fingers crossed, eh?" He looked at his watch. "I must go in a minute. Mona's making me some dinner before my late turn. Are you feeling better now?"

"Yes, thanks," Alan replied with a broad smile. "You've given me a shoulder to cry on and some hope of us working things out. What more could I ask for?"

"What are you going to do now?"

"Go to the house, I suppose. I've got to face it some time. I need to find Auntie Mary's Will and see if she left any instructions about her funeral."

"You've not been then?"

Alan shook his head. "I couldn't face it, and I still really don't want to go. Too many memories."

"Leave it for today and I'll come with you tomorrow morning."

"Davy, I can't ask you to do that."

"'Course you can. Don't be daft. I'm on late again tomorrow, so I could meet you there. What do you say? Around nine-thirty? I'm sure Mona won't mind."

"Okay, done! Thanks, Davy. That would mean a lot to me. I'll see you in the morning."

David left Alan on the moor and went home, feeling considerably more cheerful than when he'd left that morning. Seeing Alan and comforting him had helped to clarify his own thinking. It confirmed his own feelings, and the fact that Alan wanted him in his life fitted another piece of the jigsaw into place.

The best plan, he decided, was to take it one step at a time. He'd see Alan again in the morning, and the decision on the London service would be next. He would steer his way forward from there.

Veering off Course

Chapter 10

Alan

Bumping into David like that certainly improved Alan's mood. He remained where he was, sitting on the rock, for a few minutes after his friend left to go home. If he wasn't going to visit his aunt's house this afternoon, he could afford to relax a little.

The prospect of seeing David again the following morning cheered him a little and took the edge off his nervousness about visiting Auntie Mary's house. Having somebody else there would, he hoped, dull the pain, not only from the loss of his aunt and before that his parents, but also from the memories which the house held for him: the night of his first arrival as a very frightened nine-year-old, followed by his teenage years. These had on the whole been enormously happy, mainly because of David – he had such fond memories of their times there together, playing insane computer games, doing homework and watching TV. And then, finally, that last night, making gentle love to him as he had dreamed of doing for at least the three previous years.

He closed his eyes and yet another tear escaped the corner of his eye.

He stood up, shook his head as if to clear it, and set off back down the path. Time to be up and doing, he told himself, not sitting there wallowing in your own self-pity.

✛

He spent the afternoon productively, visiting a couple of undertakers and making a choice, booking the funeral for a couple of weeks' time. After that, he called in at the offices of the local newspaper and placed a notice about his aunt's death in the current week's edition, to be followed by a notice of the funeral a week later.

He returned to his hotel around four and spent the rest of the afternoon immersed in work, catching up with e-mails and making a start on a project for a client. He found the task both stimulating and diverting; it took his mind away from his loss and the unaccountably hard way in which it had hit him.

Driven from his laptop by hunger, Alan headed downstairs for dinner. He took a book with him for company but, almost inevitably, fell to reflecting upon his own situation.

The problem was that everybody left him: his parents in that blasted air crash; his grandmother a few months later, and now his aunt. Even his closest friend Tris had become more distant since he'd met Ian.

It had been Tristan's generosity that had enabled Alan to buy a home and he was hugely grateful for that but, on the whole, he would have preferred things to have stayed the way they were. No, that wasn't true; he could not begrudge Tris and Ian their happiness together, especially since he'd worked with Ian for several years and was so fond of both of them.

All of which brought him back to his Davy. In a way, even he had left him by declining to move to London six years ago and marrying Mona instead. Alan could get quite cross with him about that. The marriage had been an act of disguise rather than love, and Davy was now facing the consequences of his decision.

But Alan found it impossible to be cross with David, who was clearly anxious to do the right thing now and terrified by the possible consequences of his available courses of action. Indeed, Alan surprised himself about just how sentimental he felt about his friend. The feelings seemed to spring from nowhere after such a long time apart; they certainly did not fit his self-image. He had not been brought up to show his feelings, and his sudden outpouring of grief that morning had surprised and unnerved him.

On the other hand, being held by David whilst sitting on the moor, getting all his grief out, had felt exactly right, as right as their brief embrace in the hotel room. He remembered once again his disappointment at David's abrupt departure after they'd been out for a drink; this morning had made up for that. It had given him hope that they might grow closer in the future.

Meanwhile, he could not blame David for the decisions he'd made six years ago: it had no doubt seemed the best thing at the time. He had clearly worked very hard to make his marriage a success and was devoted to his boys. Quite what that meant for the future of any relationship between

David and him, Alan wasn't sure.

The whole thing would probably get very difficult and possibly quite nasty, he supposed. All he could do was to be there to offer love and support. The question was whether that would be enough. He fervently hoped that it would be; having rediscovered his relationship with David, he was not sure that he could stand it if it didn't work out. If somebody else walked away and left him...

He shuddered at the prospect, and forced himself to stop thinking such negative thoughts. He would see David again in the morning and for now that was enough.

Meanwhile, he needed to speak to Tris and bring him up to date about his aunt's death. He wasn't sure whether he would tell Tris about David yet. He had a feeling that Tris would not think that restarting a relationship with a married bus driver with two children was an inspired piece of decision-making.

✥

Alan walked from his hotel to his aunt's house and shivered as a bitter easterly wind swept off the moor. The previous day's glimpse of spring had been replaced by a sharp reminder that winter was not yet over. As he neared his destination, he saw David getting off the bus. They greeted each other and headed for the house round the corner.

The street was an attractive one, tree-lined, sloping gently upwards away from the town centre. The road had been laid out in the late-Victorian era, though the house itself was Edwardian. It was a terraced property, typical of millions built across the country during the decade prior to the outbreak of the First World War in 1914.

This one was stone built, with a large bay window on the ground floor. Inside there were three receptions rooms and a small kitchen on the ground floor, together with three bedrooms and a bathroom on the first floor. It had a small front garden slightly above the road, with a short flight of steps leading up to the front door.

David looked at his old friend. "Jeez, lots of memories, eh, Al?"

Alan nodded, his heart too full to allow him to speak. They stood for a moment before Alan moved to open the door. "Come on, Davy, let's do this."

He put the key in the lock and that simple act brought memories flooding back: how the lock moved and sounded; the slight creak in the hinges as it opened; the familiar smell. Eucalyptus and pine competed for their attention, as they had always done. He closed his eyes. It could have been any day of any year when he was between the ages of nine and eighteen, and he braced himself for the slightly irascible tone of Auntie Mary's voice.

The words "Alan, is that you?" had a tone about them that implied trouble; it was as if she were waiting for him to come in so she could admonish him for some sin or other, whether of omission or commission. In practice, he'd rarely been in trouble during his nine years with her. She'd been remarkably tolerant and he'd been eternally grateful, which made for a good relationship.

No, the greeting had merely been her habitual one in her usual tone of voice. Now, though, the silence was a shock, especially since everything in the place exuded a sort of spooky normality. Looking through to the kitchen,

Alan saw that her breakfast pots had been washed and left on the draining board to dry. Her shopping list was on the worktop, ready for her planned departure on the morning she'd had her first stroke.

Everything was in its correct place; the house looked much as it had when he'd left home six years before. It was more faded than he remembered, and slightly neglected; there was a light film of dust, probably inevitable since the place had lain empty for a week since his aunt had been taken off to hospital. On the sideboard, flowers in a tall vase were drooping from their age and lack of water.

There was ironing ready to do in a laundry basket. A cake tin contained a new batch of small cakes dotted with currants; they had always been his favourite and had been a staple of Auntie Mary's weekly bake for many years.

Alan felt his throat tighten once more as he saw so much that was comfortable and familiar. He was rediscovering it all, only for it to be wrenched away from him again by the passage of time and his aunt's death.

Suddenly, he felt a hand on his shoulder, squeezing. "It's all right, Al, let it go. I've got you."

He turned and looked at David, smiling into his eyes. "Thanks," he said, before sinking into David's embrace and starting to sob his heart out once again.

Chapter 11

David

"Thanks," Alan said, as he accepted a mug of tea.

"It's only dried milk," said David. "But I found it in the cupboard and thought it was better than none at all."

Alan took a sip. "It's fine, Davy. Just what the doctor ordered."

"Feeling better?"

Alan nodded. "Yes, thanks. I don't know what's the matter with me this week. I don't think I've ever been so tearful."

"It's the shock, I expect. You'd barely come to terms with the fact that she was ill and then bang, she's gone. She was a wonderful woman, too. Always very kind to me, even if she did think I was a bad influence."

"Did she? She never said that to me."

David nodded. "Aye. I'll never forget it. We'd been in trouble about something at school – I can't remember what now. But we'd had detention and were home late, and she'd been worried. She wagged her finger at me and told me that I unleashed a force in you. What did she say –

95

'I freed your imagination', that was it. Then she cuffed me round the ear and sent me home. But as I left, she threw me completely. She said, 'Never stop, Davy.' She never usually called me Davy so I was surprised. But that was it."

"She could be strange sometimes in what she said."

"I know. But that was a funny moment, you know? Anyway, there you have it – my task in life is to keep freeing your imagination." David grinned at him. "How am I doing?"

"Some dereliction of duty for the last six years, I'm afraid. But you've been doing okay this week, I think." Alan looked up from his tea and found David's eyes. "You've certainly unleashed something."

They held each other's gaze for a few moments, then David gave a small smile and an almost imperceptible nod. They remained comfortably silent whilst they finished their tea. Finally, Alan stood and reached out for David's hand. "Come on, old son, time to see what's upstairs. Let's see if we can find the Will."

Alan's old bedroom was the first room they faced when they reached the top of the stairs. It was the spacious second bedroom at the back of the house. Alan opened the door and David followed him in.

As with the kitchen, the room was completely unaltered; Auntie Mary had always kept Alan's room ready in case he ever needed to return. David looked round at the familiar posters, at a range of toys and memorabilia, including the model of the Starship Enterprise they'd made together. He felt a shiver down his spine.

In the bed there, he had spent the night with Alan before his friend left Yorkshire. They had lain together beneath those blankets and that bedspread and woken in each other's arms, knowing that they would part within the hour – possibly for ever. Now six years, one marriage and two children later, here the room was, waiting for their return. It was as if he had made a journey backwards in time. If only he could – that would enable him to put right all the mistakes he had made.

As they stood there, David felt Alan's hand slide into his own. He gripped Alan's fingers and squeezed. Now it was his turn to be overcome by the power of the moment. He felt his lip tremble slightly and his eyes fill. When he spoke, his voice was rough with emotion.

"Oh, God, Al. I'm so sorry."

Alan chuckled but then caught sight of his friend's expression. "Hey, Davy, whatever for?"

"For being such a fucking coward. I should have come with you that morning but I was so scared, Al. I'd just had the best night of my life. Looking back, I can't believe that I couldn't see what was staring me in the face."

"Davy, it was never that simple. You mustn't blame yourself. It was scary stuff – expecting you to cope with what had happened between us and up sticks and move 200 miles away. It simply wasn't on."

"I dare say, but I *knew*, Al. I knew that what we had felt right and that you were more than my best pal. Even if I couldn't come with you there and then, I didn't have to run off and get *married*, for fuck's sake."

Alan gave a small huff. "No, I suppose not. But I absolutely understand why you did it and there's no need to apologise – least of all to me."

"I suppose not, but oh... Coming back here brings it all

back, all those years of friendship and feeling safe ... all gone, Al. All gone." A wave of nostalgia swept over him and almost carried him away: the tears returned with a vengeance and escaped down his cheeks.

He found himself enveloped in a hug and relaxed into the embrace, burying his face in Alan's neck. Alan's hand rubbed his back and the movement comforted and helped to calm him. He started to feel better, but found himself very unwilling to let go. He did not want to break the moment. A warm feeling spread through his body as, once again, he experienced that feeling of *rightness* that he had just been talking about, and which was his strongest memory from their night together.

Alan's head moved and he kissed David on the temple. "Better now?" he asked.

David nodded, and pulled his head back to look Alan in the eye. "Thanks, much better."

But still he didn't let go, revelling in the warmth and security of their embrace. Alan inclined his head a little closer until their lips brushed against each other. The kiss deepened and built steadily from tentative to passionate. David did not bolt this time.

Within moments, they were both naked and clamped together, moving their bodies in unison while they kissed passionately. Alan manoeuvred David on top of himself and opened his legs wide to accommodate his lower body. He wrapped his legs round David's hips to draw him in as close as possible.

"Oh, God, Davy, I missed you so much."

David was momentarily nonplussed, but suddenly realised that this explained so much about Alan's behaviour over the last couple of days. He was about to think that through when another kiss distracted him.

Alan whispered, "I want you to fuck me, Davy. Will you do that for me? I need to feel you inside me."

David felt a shiver of anticipation. He lifted his head and looked Alan in the eye. "Bloody hell, Al. You sure?"

Alan nodded. "I've dreamt of it for six years."

"So that's a 'yes' then. I'd be honoured. But you'll have to help me, show me how. I wouldn't want to hurt you."

Alan grinned up at him. "You won't do that, I promise. Not if we're careful." He lifted his head from the pillow and kissed David on the end of his nose. "Come on then. Lesson one – reach for my wallet, if you can see it. There's a sachet of lube and a condom in there."

Under his lover's expert guidance, David prepared him using his fingers first. The lessons were punctuated by kisses and fondling, all of which meant that by the time Alan whispered, "Now, Davy. I need you inside me," they were both coiled like springs.

David pushed Alan's legs back over his chest to gain better access. Slowly, slowly, he pushed his way in, whilst Alan worked hard to relax and welcome him. Once he was fully home, David relaxed. The sensation was more intense than anything he had ever felt before. The warmth that was generated by their connection seemed to spread through his whole body, like coming home to a coal fire on a winter's night.

"God, Al, that's incredible. You're so tight! It feels so good."

"You can move now. I'm okay."

David moved out very slowly and in again, generating

a whole new set of sensations that almost took his breath away. He did it again, and then again, steadily building up a rhythm that had Alan squirming and panting for more. David reached down for a kiss, after which Alan reached for his own erection to pump in time with David's thrusts. Their pace got steadily faster; Alan's whimpers were almost continuous. His orgasm hit and he shot all over his chest and stomach. At the same time, he clamped down on David inside him, which took David over the edge too. David's body spasmed and he surrendered to the sensations he was feeling, crying out Alan's name.

After a few moments, David pulled out gently and lay sideways on the bed, struggling to recover his breath. He drew Alan into an embrace and kissed him. "Christ, Al – that was... Wow!"

"Yeah, it was, Davy. I've never...' Alan paused.

"Never what?"

"I've never known anything so intense," he resumed. "Thank you."

After a few minutes, they cleaned themselves up and dressed again, before lying back on the bed, close together but not touching.

"I ought to go soon," said David eventually. "Mona's expecting me for my dinner before I go to work." He grinned, "I've not been much help to you with the house, I'm afraid."

"You've been more help than you could possibly know, Davy. You got me through the front door – I'm not at all sure that I could have done that on my own. And now this, back together in this bed. Whatever else happens, we'll always have the memory of this to treasure."

Chapter 12

Alan

David left the house a few minutes later, promising to return the following day if he could to help sort the house out.

Alan was determined to focus on the task in hand rather than what had just happened. He would have time later to process those events and think about what might happen next. For now, the important thing was dealing with his aunt's affairs.

Having waved David off after a long, lingering kiss in the hall, Alan went back upstairs to his aunt's bedroom. He had a distant memory of her papers being kept in a bureau in the far alcove of the room to the right of the chimney breast.

Entering the room, he was almost overpowered by the smell of eucalyptus and again struck by the appearance of normality: bed neatly made; nightdress folded on the pillow; make-up and hairbrushes neatly arranged on the dressing table. His aunt's favourite perfume was there as well – the source of the eucalyptus smell in the room.

Going in there, seeing the room as if Auntie Mary had just left it, he felt rather like one of the sailors who had discovered the *Marie Celeste* must have done. Except there was no mystery here; he knew what had happened to his aunt. The problem was that, in this room, he could not quite believe it.

Sure enough, the bureau was still in the alcove as he remembered it. Sliding back the cover, he found what he expected: a neatly arranged set of cubby holes and the keys to the drawers.

After a few moments, he had everything that he needed – his aunt's Will, a schedule of her investments, and lists of contact information and account details. Her long training as a secretary had spilled over into her personal life.

Looking at the investments, and bearing in mind the likely value of the house, it looked as if the estate would be worth a bob or two. Alan knew that he was the sole beneficiary, so he would be comfortably off at the end of the process. He shook his head; he would trade all of this new wealth for another day or two of his aunt's company and the chance to thank her for all she had done for him.

Armed with the documents, he spent the rest of the afternoon on the phone. He made appointments over the next few days with her solicitor, bank manager and financial adviser. When five o'clock came, he'd had enough and headed back to the hotel for a shower and a drink ... and a long think.

✛

The shower took longer than he'd anticipated. As soon as

he undressed, he recalled what it had been like to be naked in David's arms. That aroused him again, and he spent time in languorous contemplation of what they had done together. He revelled particularly in the memory of how David had felt inside him, how beautiful he had looked when he came. That brought Alan to another shattering climax and left him feeling even more drained.

After a while, he roused himself and headed downstairs for dinner. He took his book again but, as with the previous evening, he found it difficult to concentrate. His mind was too full and moved rapidly from one topic to another – his inheritance, missing his aunt, his time with Davy this morning, what his life might bring, his time with Davy this morning, what was next with his career, his time with...

Despite all the uncertainties, he could not help but feel optimistic about the future. He was about to achieve a degree of financial security most people only dreamed of; he already had a good job, a smart car and a flat that was both comfortable and convenient. He would see Davy from time to time – more, if the London bus service came off. He didn't know whether that would be enough for either of them as they rekindled their friendship and hopefully took it to the next stage but, if what they had was to go anywhere, he had to be patient and move at David's pace. David was the one facing the difficult decisions and the trauma of a marriage breakdown. The poor lad would need love and support, not nagging from the side lines.

As he sat over his coffee, his mobile pinged with a message from the man himself.

DAVID:> Really sorry. Not going to be able to make tomorrow. Tommy had a fall. Currently in A&E.

ALAN:> Understood. Don't worry. Is he OK?
DAVID:> Cuts and bruises. Poorly ankle, maybe sprain or break.
ALAN:> Fingers crossed. Be safe.

✛

The time until Auntie Mary's funeral passed very quickly. Alan was fully occupied with the house, sorting out her affairs and keeping up with e-mails and messages from the office.

David was also fully occupied and they only managed one brief meeting in the café where they'd sat that first day at the end of David's shift. Tommy had indeed fractured his ankle in a fall whilst playing in the garden. Life was hectic as David and Mona managed their home and looked after Kevin, in addition to making hospital visits and coping with Tommy's absence from school.

Their meeting was severely constrained; neither of them could say out loud what they were feeling in such a public place. There was virtually no physical contact between them – merely covert brushing of thighs under the table.

"I'm not going to be able to make the funeral, Al. I'm really sorry."

"Don't worry, Davy. I understand. It's one of those things. I shall miss you, though."

There was a pause, about the tenth in five minutes.

"When are you planning to go back to London?" David asked.

"Tomorrow afternoon, after the service. I must get back to work, there's a client meeting the day after tomorrow and I simply have to be there. I've arranged to ship all the bits of furniture I want and the house clearance people will come on Monday. Hilda Rodgerson – you know, the next-door neighbour – is going to let them in for me. As soon as that's done, the house can go on the market."

"Gosh, that's quick, Al."

"I know, but it's the best way. I don't want to have to keep coming back, and most of the stuff has no value."

"All those memories."

"I know, Davy, I know." Alan grinned. "We'll just have to make some more when you come to London. Any news on that, by the way?"

David shook his head. "Not so far. I'll let you know as soon as I hear."

"God, I hope it all works out, Davy."

"Me too. I don't know what I'd do if... Well, you know."

"We'll work it out, come what may. Now that I've found you again, I'm not letting go."

His own vehemence surprised Alan, so he tried to lighten the mood with a smile. Under the table, he reached for David's hand and gave it a squeeze. He saw David's eyes moisten and felt his own do the same.

"Time for my next trip, I think," said David reluctantly, rising from the table. "I hope everything goes okay tomorrow. I'll be thinking of you. Keep in touch."

"Thanks. I will, Davy. Promise." Alan suddenly recalled their school days. "Cross my heart and hope to die."

David responded immediately. "Stick a needle in my eye." He left the café with a grin on his face.

Veering off Course

Chapter 13

David

The delivery of six brand new coaches to Sedgethwaite's Leeds Road depot in early April caused quite a stir. It was some years since the company's coaching activities had been handed to a fellow company in a reorganisation so the appearance of these high-specification, twin-deck vehicles, complete with toilet, attracted a lot of interest from staff, public and the local press.

The arrival of the coaches coincided with the announcement of the names of the men who would drive the new London service. An earlier decision had been delayed by a dispute between management and the trade union over the selection method. The union committee had decided to push for selection on the basis of seniority only, but management insisted that the prime criterion should be suitability. When the two sides failed to agree, a union branch meeting was held, ostensibly to agree to 'black' the coaches – in other words, to refuse to drive them. However, the committee, much to their chagrin, was outvoted, primarily by the younger men who were anxious for a crack at the long-distance work and were not prepared to see it reserved for the older men. Members of the committee noted that it had been the best attended branch meeting for years and commented sourly upon a lack of solidarity for the cause.

It all made for an unpleasant atmosphere in the depot for several days, and David did not endear himself to the union branch chairman, Douggie Thorpe. Now approaching sixty, Douggie had been around when David's grandad was working. As a result, and following an appeal to historic loyalties, he'd been disappointed when David refused to back the committee's appeal.

"Look, Douggie," David tried to explain. "The committee decided on their line without actually asking anybody – and the seniority argument almost exclusively favours your cronies. So why should you be surprised if the younger guys resent it?"

"But what we're saying is custom and practice – it's what we've always done."

"That's as may be, Douggie, but these days custom and practice won't wash with a lot of the lads."

Douggie had let the matter go but not before issuing a warning. "You might need the shop stewards to help you one day, and then what will happen?"

David reported for work, unaware that the great announcement was about to be made. One part of him wanted to get on to the rota and knew that his best chance was if the younger element in the workforce won. But – other than the discussion with Douggie Thorpe – he had not got involved in the arguments that had raged hourly in the canteen. Deep down, another part of him hoped that he could avoid temptation by not being selected.

He'd always been a fairly unobtrusive employee, keeping his own counsel and coming and going every day without making much of an impact. Even so, he felt that he was part of the place. Now he realised that was becoming less and less true: he felt himself increasingly isolated from his colleagues and their concerns. He was bored with the talk of women, beer and football, and fed up with the sight of women's tits on as many pages of the newspapers as their editors thought they could get away with.

What made it even worse was the fact that he felt the same at home. He was out of sympathy with his wife's devotion to television, and to soap operas in particular, but he had no positive alternative to offer. He spent a lot of time in the garden and still enjoyed playing with the boys, but his home life had all lost any sense of permanence.

Mona chatted away happily about his prospects of becoming an inspector and about them buying a house in the autumn. David joined in the conversations, but he no longer shared his wife's dreams or her belief that they would come true. He knew that it was cruel to let her carry on assuming that he still shared her aspirations – but he did not have the courage to disabuse her.

The sense of impending change, of transition, would have been tolerable if he had known what was likely to happen next, or how to precipitate the change. It was as if he had visited a clairvoyant who'd said that his life would be transformed but then refused to go further. Meanwhile, his predominant feeling was of loneliness and isolation, which made him moody and introspective.

The notice was posted around mid-morning and was

up in the bus station canteen when David returned from his last trip to Leeds. There was a cluster round the notice board as he entered the room. When they greeted him as one of the 'Sedgethwaite Flyers', he knew he had been selected.

He laughed gently as various people kidded him but inwardly his heart leapt. Surely this was a sign and he would now be shown the way forward? He pulled out his phone and sent Alan a quick text to let him know.

Chapter 14

Alan

Alan received David's text whilst he was lunching with his friend Tristram. It was a strange quirk of fate that it arrived at that moment, since it was the occasion when he'd planned to tell Tris what had happened in Sedgethwaite. It had not seemed right to talk about it over the phone, and circumstances had conspired to keep them out of each other's company for three or four weeks.

Alan could not disguise his pleasure as he read the text, nor prevent himself from saying 'Brilliant' out loud.

"Good news?" asked Tris

"The best," Alan replied. He paused for a moment, before adding, "I think."

"Come on, spill the beans," said Tris. "This is about what happened while you were in Sedgethwaite, isn't it?"

Alan nodded.

"I knew it. I could tell that something was up, other than your aunt."

"Who was down. And out."

"Ew, gross, Alan."

"Sorry. Couldn't resist it."

"So stop stalling. What happened?"

"You remember me telling you about David, my old school pal?"

"Oh yeah. Didn't you two hook up immediately before you came to London?"

"Yeah, right. The thing is, I bumped into him again."

"Really? How did you manage that?"

"I got on his bus."

Tris laughed. "That's almost as good as me falling over you in The Salisbury!"

"Quite. Anyway, it was good to see him again. We were very close, you know, for a very long time."

"I remember. So what happened?"

"Well, we went for a cuppa and I met him for a drink in the evening."

"And?"

"He came back to the hotel with me."

"Alan...' There was a warning note in Tris's voice. "Didn't you tell me that he'd got married?"

"Yup. They have two boys."

"Crikey. What happened?"

"Nothing. He kissed me but then bailed out. But I bumped into him again the next day, after my aunt had died. He comforted me and told me..."

"Told you what?" asked Tris. "God, it's like getting blood out of a stone."

"That he'd made a mistake in getting married and should have come to London with me."

"Oh."

"Anyway, he helped me when I had to go to my aunt's

house, and we … um … got together."

"And?"

"So he's got a job driving coaches to London. He'll be staying overnight every now and again."

"With you, presumably?"

Alan nodded. "Thing is, Tris, I think he probably means as much to me now as he ever did."

"Really?"

"Yes. I've realised since I saw him again that he's been my soulmate ever since I met him at the age of nine."

"Christ, Alan. Why do I have a sinking feeling? You realise that this probably isn't going to end well?"

"I know what you mean. After all, it's lesson one in the Gay 101 course, isn't it? Don't date married men."

"I'm sure there must be examples of relationships that start like that working out, but I've never heard of any."

"Neither have I," Alan responded gloomily. "Though I suppose this is a bit different. We are very old friends, after all, and it's not some grand experiment."

"I hope you're right. But two kids, Alan? How on earth is that going to work?"

Alan shrugged. "The short answer is that I've no idea – and I don't suppose Davy has either. We've not got that far. All I know is that I was bloody glad to see him again. Being with him made me feel whole again in a way I haven't done for six years. I'd be mad to throw away any chance of a future like that, however slim it might be."

"I can understand that, Alan. After all, it's what Ian and I have, and we've you to thank for it. Please don't think that I'm out to judge you or interfere in any way. I worry about you getting hurt, that's all. I know that you're not as tough as you like to pretend."

"No, I get that, I really do. And about the vulnerability. I hadn't realised it until last week. It freaked me out a bit, to be honest." Alan shook his head, disbelievingly. "I suppose it was Auntie Mary dying so suddenly. I felt so damned lonely up there and I got a bit tearful – well, more than a bit. It scared me. I'd not felt like that since Mum and Dad were killed."

"I can understand that. Somebody else leaving you in the lurch?"

Alan looked up and gave Tris a rueful smile. "You know me too well, old son. You're right. I realised the other day that a tiny part of me feels the same about you, getting together with Ian. Stupid, I know, but I suppose we can't help our feelings."

"No, that's true. But about Ian and me, you must realise that you're part of our family. We'll always be there for you."

"Thanks, Tris. Deep down I know that but sometimes, you know, in the watches of the night...'

"Oh, I know that feeling, all right."

"Exactly. Anyway, the point is I've got to be strong for the next few months, for Davy's sake. I need to be the person he can turn to. So I'll rely on you two for support – and Simon and Peter as well."

"Yes, I really like those two guys – you fell on your feet when you bought the flat and found them as your downstairs neighbours. Don't worry, Alan, the four of us have got your back."

"Thanks."

"So when do I get to meet him, your Davy?"

"Soon, I hope. He starts on the new London service next month."

Veering off Course

Chapter 15

David

"Right, pull into this service area and we'll let young Edgeley take over."

David and his colleagues were on a training run to London. It was the second time he'd driven one of the coaches, and he almost felt more nervous this time than he'd been on his familiarisation day the previous week. Driving a forty-feet long vehicle was bad enough, even round areas that you knew well, but on the motorway... That was – well, pretty awesome.

They pulled into the service area and took a short break. Then it was off again towards London with David at the wheel. The training inspector sat in the courier seat and chatted comfortably. "Okay, fine. Build your speed up gradually. Get accustomed to it, and to the note of the engine. Right, it should change into top about ... now."

David felt the automatic gears shift and immediately felt better. His vision was superb, and the vehicle rode beautifully.

"Now, you're going to overtake that lorry, so you want

to be out early. Remember that you're not driving a car – you've got to pull out early to make sure you're straight when overtaking. And it also makes the passengers' life easier because they aren't spending the whole journey expecting you to bump into the vehicle in front."

David pulled into the middle lane and allowed the coach to accelerate again. He was doing around fifty-five by now and felt very much in control. He allowed his speed to build towards the maximum sixty-two miles an hour and started to relax a little, enjoying the sensation of speed.

They had spent the journey so far going over ticketing and luggage procedures. The idea was that they would go right through to Victoria to see what happened there and what to do about parking the coach up during their break or on an overnight run. Afterwards they would drive straight back to learn the northward route out of London. It would be a long day, but a very useful one.

David had not realised how much of his present job had become instinctive; there was a great deal to re-learn for a different type of service. And different this certainly would be, with luggage to look after, the tickets all being sold online, and a toilet to keep an eye on. They'd come a long way from his uncle's day, when a coach journey from Sedgethwaite to London took fourteen hours!

He had not seen Alan since their brief meeting the day before Auntie Mary's funeral; their only contact had been a couple of text messages over David's selection for the London route. Now the service was starting, he would have to put that right. The thought of seeing Alan again gave him butterflies in his stomach. Maybe that, rather than the change of job, would really mark the start of a new chapter in his life.

"Right, that's fast enough, young man."

The instructor's voice brought him back to the present and he realised that he had hit the maximum speed on the limiter. He forced himself to concentrate on the task in hand. For the moment, the future could look after itself.

David drove the rest of the way into London. It was his first experience of London traffic and he found it a little terrifying, but he managed to get the vehicle into Victoria unscathed. Leaving there, they were shown the route to the overnight park before heading back to the coach station. They were given an hour's break before setting off back north.

David set off for a quick wander round, with the instructor's words about accommodation ringing in his ears. "Most of you will use the regular digs near the coach station. I'm told they're not bad, though it's many years since I used them myself. But of course, you don't have to. Quite a few lads have got relatives or friends around London, and staying with them can often be quite useful 'cos you'll still get your overnight allowance, of course."

David was amused. So, staying the odd night with Alan would make him some money as well as everything else that might happen. He shivered with pleasure at the thought – and at that moment walked straight into him.

"Hey watch where you're... Good God. Davy! Whatever are you doing down here?"

"Alan! I was just thinking about you! What are *you* doing round here?"

"I told you I worked near the coach station. Don't you remember?"

"Oh, aye, I'd forgotten. I'm down on a training run – we start properly next week. I was going to text you as soon as I knew when my first overnight was due."

"That's fantastic, Davy. I'll look forward to that. Have you got time for a pie and a pint? I was on my way to lunch. There's a place round the corner."

David grinned. "Aye, that would be grand. I've got about half an hour. But no alcohol, mind. Not this time. I'm driving."

"Fancy! My Davy driving one of those big coaches."

David laughed and bumped his shoulder, but inside he felt a little warm glow from Alan calling him "my Davy".

✛

David Edgeley shut the front door quietly and set off down the hill. The pavements glistened with a late frost and he shivered in the pre-dawn cold. He noticed the steam from his breath and hoped that the staff bus was running on time.

It began to get light as he reached the bus stop. It might be a good omen, he thought; perhaps the sun was going to shine on his first solo trip to London.

A distant growl announced that Jim was coaxing one of the depot's older buses up the hill. David glanced at his watch; only a couple of minutes late. Not bad, especially for the second run!

Pat Eckersley had gone on the earlier run, so David was able to settle down without the customary banter. Everybody else was quiet, coming to terms with the start of another day. At the depot, they piled into the office to greet the depot inspector.

"Morning, Jack."

"Morning, young David. No need to ask what you're on."

David grinned. "First London, Inspector," he said with mock formality.

"Aye. You've got number 501. Now behave yourself down there, lad. I don't want your Mona coming round here blaming me for any trouble."

David laughed, but not at quite the same aspect of the joke as Jack Davis. "No worries there, Jack. I'll behave."

He left the depot office and went to collect his coach. This was not an overnight duty; they would be making the three-fifteen back from London, so his next meeting with Alan would have to wait for a few days. But their chance meeting at lunchtime the previous week had been great. Fate was quite clearly on Alan's side, and seeing him again had reinforced David's conviction about where his future lay.

The new service confirmed its potential when, on only the second morning, David picked up a good thirty passengers in the bus station. A few minutes later, David swung the coach round a roundabout, down the slip road and onto the Ml motorway. As he settled down to a cruising speed, he flicked the switch of the PA.

"Good morning, ladies and gentlemen, and welcome aboard the London service. My name is David, and I'm your driver. We are now on the M1 Motorway. We shall be arriving in London at about twelve-thirty. I would like to remind you that there is a toilet at the rear of the vehicle. Please consider your fellow passengers when using your phone or listening to music. I hope you enjoy your experience of our new service."

Filtering into the stream of traffic, David smirked a little at his own words. "Not as much as I will."

✥

As April drifted into a warm early May, Sedgethwaite's new coach service settled into a routine. Passenger numbers went from strength to strength, attracted by low fares and internet booking.

David found coach driving interesting and challenging. He particularly enjoyed interacting with the passengers, though he recognised that motorway driving might eventually become tedious and boring.

His first overnight trip was during the second week of operation. Mona continued to insist that she wasn't worried about being left on her own with the boys. David had a couple of stolen phone conversations with Alan, in which they made arrangements to meet up, alongside a certain amount of flirting and joking around. Thus it was that David left Sedgethwaite at two-thirty in the afternoon, looking forward to his first night away from home for many years.

All went smoothly and the journey was trouble-free. They pulled into Victoria dead on time and David took the coach across the river to the overnight coach park. They'd arranged for Alan to meet him at the coach park this time so David could get his bearings.

As he pulled the empty vehicle in, drove through the wash, fuelled and parked it, he felt nervous. He would be seeing Alan again, visiting his flat for the first time, spending the night there... These were new and exciting experiences but also a bit scary, outside his comfort zone. For a start, he was in London, more than 200 miles from home, from anything he'd ever known. Meeting his old pal again in Sedgethwaite had been easy; he was on home territory, surrounded by known landmarks and recognisable streets. Even at Auntie Mary's house, everything had been familiar. Now, though, who knew?

Then he dismissed his fears. This was Alan. His Al, his friend for seventeen and more years. What could possibly go wrong?

He shook his head, got out of the cab and headed for the exit to the coach park. He turned out of the gate and there was a familiar figure, standing by a stylish BMW.

David plastered a grin on his face and stepped forward to meet his buddy.

Veering off Course

Chapter 16

Alan

Alan's flat was a new conversion at the top of a Victorian house. It was spacious, cheerful and bright, helped by the high ceilings, cheerful decorations and modern furniture.

It was clear that David was impressed. Alan followed him from room to room, amused by his friend's enthusiasm for what he had come to take for granted. Not having seen the Edgeley household, he had no point of comparison – but he could guess what David's home was like.

Eventually, he managed to slow David down long enough to haul him into a hug and kiss him. "I'm glad you like it."

"It's really great, Al. I don't think I've ever seen a place that looks so … well, cheerful."

"What about me? Aren't I really great too, Davy?"

"Of course, you daft bugger. Taken as read."

They kissed again, longer and harder. "Welcome to my home, Davy, and welcome back into my life."

"You say the nicest things, Al."

Allan pulled away. "Food," he said, breaking their embrace and heading down the short flight of stairs to the half-landing where the kitchen was. "There you are, having driven such a big vehicle all the way from Yorkshire. You must be starving. Come and eat."

As soon as the date had been set and the details finalised, Alan had gone into panic mode. He had worried for several days about how to strike the right note. Should they go out or stay in, cook at home or get take away? And if he cooked, what to have – exotic or basic?

He had entered into lengthy consultations with his friends and downstairs neighbours, Simon and Peter, and consulted Tris as well. Eventually, they had all agreed that staying in would be a good idea and that Alan should cook. Something simple but classic, like pasta. He chose lasagne because it was flexible – the final cooking could be postponed if David were delayed – and besides everybody loved it. He'd chosen a bottle of Valpolicella to go with it.

The meal seemed to be a great success. David made appreciative noises as he ate, a sort of humming sound as he chewed, a trait that Alan remembered from childhood days, which filled him with nostalgia.

Despite his obvious enjoyment of the food, though, David's mood seemed to darken as the evening wore on. He smiled less often and became less talkative. He was no less affectionate, and obviously found it difficult if there was no physical contact of some sort between them, but still the mood darkened. The teasing and little jokes with which they had started the evening disappeared.

After the meal, Alan made coffee, not a cup of instant in a mug but real coffee, from a filter machine, served in a cup. They took the coffee and the rest of the wine upstairs to the sitting room. Alan turned the lights down low and put on some music quietly in the background.

He pointed Davy in the direction of the sofa, sat down in the chair opposite and looked closely at his friend. "Well?" he asked.

"Well what?" David responded.

"You've got quieter and quieter as the evening's gone on. Are you okay?"

"More than. I've had a lovely time, Al, and the meal was great."

"Why do I sense a 'but' coming?"

David shook his head. "No 'buts'. Your flat is lovely. The lasagne was great. I liked the wine, and the coffee. Oh, and the music too. It's just ... so different, that's all."

"Different from what, Davy?"

"My life. Your past. Everything. Where on earth would you find a place like this on Beckett's Hill estate? It makes me..." He paused, groping for the word.

"Jealous?"

"No, no. That's not it at all. It saddens me, because it makes me realise how narrow my life is, and how much I'm missing. I should've come with you, Al, all those years ago. I'm sorry I didn't. I feel so ignorant, so out of my depth." Suddenly David's eyes filled and a stray tear found its way down his cheek.

Alan moved across to the sofa and put his arm round David's shoulder. "Hey, you mustn't be upset. Tonight isn't about making you feel inferior or bad about yourself – it's about having fun, enjoying ourselves, like we always used to. The location's different and the ingredients might have changed a bit, but it's still *us*. We haven't changed – it's still Al and Davy having a good time. And you must admit that we were always bloody good at that."

David laughed at that and briskly wiped away the tears. "Aye, that's bloody reight."

Alan squeezed his friend's shoulders and kissed him on the temple. Slightly surprised at the gesture, David turned to look at him. The look Alan saw in his eyes melted his heart and he leaned forward for a kiss.

After a few moments, David broke away and again looked into his friend's eyes. "Oh, Al," he said. "What the fuck am I going to do?"

Chapter 17

David

"Good morning, ladies and gentlemen, and welcome aboard this West Yorkshire express service to Sedgethwaite. My name is David and I am your driver...'

David finished his welcome announcement and started the journey north. Within a few minutes, he was pushing his coach through Hyde Park Corner and swinging into Park Lane. Another journey was under way. Once again they had a good load – the coach was about three-quarters full, which was good going. It was a lovely day and it promised to be a smooth ride. With luck, he would get an hour or two in the garden this afternoon. One of the big advantages of his job was that it freed him up to do other things during the day, either after an early turn or before a late one. That way, you didn't spend your entire life working – unless you did huge amounts of overtime, of course.

During the ride up Finchley Road, David spent his time remembering Alan's flat – how stylish it was, and how much he wanted to live somewhere like that, rather than in a dingy council house in Sedgethwaite.

They reached Golders Green and picked up more customers before setting off north again and joining the motorway. The traffic was fairly quiet, so David had more time to think.

Memories of the previous night crowded in on him. He had been bowled over with Alan's apartment from the moment he'd arrived. He'd compared the decoration with Mona's taste for lively wallpaper with big patterns; he'd looked at the furniture and thought of their own cheap, vinyl-covered suite, which had been both fashionable and affordable when they'd bought it when he and Mona moved into the Beckett's Hill house. It now looked worn and shabby.

The other thing that had impressed David about the flat were the house plants; they were a revelation, giving the living room a life that its plain painted walls would not otherwise have had.

Not to mention the delicious food, the wine and Alan's charm as a host, which seemed so effortless. It had all fascinated David. To him, pasta was something you ate out of a packet or in a foreign restaurant – it wasn't the sort of food you made at home, especially not cooked by a *man*. He certainly had not known what Valpolicella was; if he'd been asked, he would have said it involved wallpaper paste rather than red wine.

The music Alan had played was unfamiliar but David liked the tune. What was the composer's name? Yes, Mozart, wasn't it. That rang a bell from his mum, who sometimes listened to Classic FM on the radio. He would remember the taste of the coffee for ever; he had been bowled over by the intensity of its flavour.

Far more than the way he dressed, and drinking wine in the pub, it was the flat and the meal that showed David how far Alan had moved from his Yorkshire upbringing. This was a totally different world, a way of life as far removed from David's as a Frenchman's or a Spaniard's. The gap between their lives and experience was now so wide that, when you thought about it, the two of them actually had very little in common save their shared memories.

Yet it hadn't felt like that. They had relaxed again; they had chatted, joked, laughed and taken the mickey out of each other exactly as they had always done when they were kids. Being with Alan just felt *right* – as instinctive as cleaning your teeth every morning.

Of all the events of the visit, the one that stood out in David's memory was sleeping with Alan in his bed. They had not had sex – somehow the question had not arisen – but lain together, wrapped in each other's arms, kissing languidly on occasion, enjoying the comfort of being with each other. After a while, they both fell asleep; they had awoken in exactly the same position when Alan's alarm clock had rung. Neither of them spoke much as they got ready for work but their farewell was tender – another gentle kiss from Alan.

"Bye bye, Davy. See you next week. And thanks for last night."

"What for? It's me that should be thanking you. I had a great time."

"I dare say, but thanks anyway. Just holding you this time was … well, a bit special."

Suddenly, a patch of roadworks was looming and it broke

Davy's train of thought. Forced to concentrate on the road ahead, he dismissed his memories.

Chapter 18

Alan

David's second overnight visit to the Clapham flat was scheduled to take place the following week. This time he would make his own way to the flat, whilst Alan would again cook them a meal.

Although he was less nervous this time, Alan was nevertheless anxious that everything should go as smoothly as possible. But what he had not allowed for when they had planned these visits was the pressure on them that their enforced separation would generate. Nine days was a long time to be apart at this stage in a relationship; as a result, their need for each other was reaching almost feral proportions.

Consequently, when Alan opened the door to his flat to find David on the threshold, food was the last thing on either of their minds. On that first occasion, their embraces had been comforting and the kisses gentle; this time, their visceral need for each other overrode any restraint.

David stepped across the threshold straight into Alan's welcoming arms and their lips collided in a long, passionate kiss. Somehow, Alan managed to manoeuvre them both up two flights of stairs without their lips breaking contact.

Once in the bedroom, clothes were removed at some speed whilst they continued to kiss passionately. Once they were undressed, Alan manoeuvred them on to the bed, with David on top, wrapping both arms and legs round him, as if to draw him in completely.

Alan closed his eyes and sighed deeply at the sheer joy of the sensations he was experiencing – the warmth of another body, the touch of somebody else's skin, the comfort of being held, the taste of David's lips and tongue. They resumed their kissing, clinging on to each other like drowning men. Eventually Alan pulled away slightly, needing to breathe. "Oh, God, Davy, I've missed you so much."

David was momentarily nonplussed but suddenly realised that this explained so much about Alan's welcome tonight. He was about to think that through when another kiss distracted him. This was followed by a whisper in his ear. "I want you to fuck me again tonight, Davy. Will you do that for me? I need to feel you inside me again."

Alan watched for David's reaction and saw him shiver with anticipation. He lifted his head and looked Alan in the eye. "God, yes!" he replied. "I've dreamed of doing this again, ever since that day in your old room. But I'm still a bit scared of doing it wrong, of hurting you."

Alan tightened his grip and looked up at him. "You won't hurt me, Davy. Promise." He flipped them over so that he lay on top. "But this time I'm going to ride my sexy coach driver."

He saw David's eyes widen with surprise and interest.

"How does that work, then?"

"Ah, you'll see," Alan replied with a grin.

As on the first occasion, David prepared him carefully with his fingers, once more under Alan's expert guidance. The preparation was punctuated by more kisses and stroking. Alan's touch on David's skin was feather-light at times, making him wriggle with pleasure and let out a small, growling sound.

Alan laughed. "I'd swear, David Edgeley, that you were a cat in a previous life. You're positively purring."

David gave a short giggle. "Yes, I do love to be stroked. Especially by big toms like you."

Matters became more serious again. After a few moments, Alan reached for the lube and readied both of them. He sat up and straddled David, reaching behind him to guide David's cock into place. Alan leant backwards and bore downwards, allowing David to enter him and slide smoothly into place. He rested for a moment to allow his body to adjust, and felt a thrill as David let out an involuntary moan.

"Oh, Al, that feels amazing. It's so ... so incredible. I never thought I could feel this good."

Alan began to move up and down, swivelling his hips at the same time. He closed his eyes to luxuriate in the sensations he was feeling, then leaned down for a kiss. As they broke apart, David opened his eyes and looked into Alan's for a few moments. His friend's pupils were blown and he seemed to be having difficulty focussing. He looked so sexy in that position.

Alan sat up and began to move once more. The change in angle meant that David's cock brushed his prostate, causing him to cry out with pleasure. He held the angle and received this intense burst of pleasure on each thrust. His orgasm started to build, helped along by David, who reached up, seized him and stroked in time with Alan's movement.

Their pace began to build and the room was filled with the noise of their cries. Alan's orgasm hit and he shot all over David's chest and stomach. At the same time, his involuntary spasm took David to the edge. As in Sedgethwaite a couple of weeks earlier, David's whole body spasmed. He completely lost control as his limbs twitched and he yelled Alan's name.

After a few moments, Alan lifted himself off David carefully and dropped down onto the mattress next to him. They lay side by side, gasping to recover their breath.

Alan turned on his side and drew David into an embrace and kissed him. As they broke the kiss, David let out a short laugh. "I didn't think it could get any better than the first time but it just did."

"I know, Davy. That was ... breath-taking."

"Thanks. For me too."

They lay still for a few minutes, needing to recover their equilibrium and to come to terms with the depth of feeling that their act of love had created.

Chapter 19

David

Any lingering doubts that David might have had about what he and Alan were doing were swept away on the tide of emotion that welled up during and immediately after his orgasm. He now knew absolutely that he could not go back to his old life. He belonged here, and Alan was his. With that at the front of his mind, he reached over and kissed him once more.

Alan might have been the more experienced of the two of them in the art of gay sex, but he would not have claimed to be the world's greatest expert. In fact, if tonight was anything to go by, he had huge amounts more to learn and to practise. And the practice may as well begin here and now. He responded to David's sweet kiss with a more passionate one of his own.

But his own stomach chose that moment to grumble loudly, closely followed by David's. It was time for food rather than sex. He broke away. "Come on, young Davy, it's time we fed our faces."

However, they needed to shower first, so Alan headed for the bathroom, quickly followed by David. Sadly there was not enough room for them both in there together... Showered and dressed in loose clothing, Alan went to the kitchen and put the final touches to the dish he had prepared.

✛

"I could definitely get used to your cooking, Al. That was fantastic."

Alan had cooked a simple baked dish of pasta, gammon and leek in cheese sauce. The combination of flavours had David humming with pleasure – it was another new food experience that he thoroughly enjoyed. Once again, though, it brought into sharp relief the contrast between their lifestyles; Mona would not have dreamt of cooking gammon without chips and egg.

"Where on earth did you learn to cook like this? As I recall, you couldn't even boil an egg when we were teenagers."

"I'll have you know that my Auntie Mary had taught me to do a very fine boiled egg, David Edgeley. I could scramble them as well."

David sniggered. "Well, you certainly know how to scramble mine."

Alan puffed himself with pretend indignation. "I don't know. Insults my culinary skills and then utters such filth in my kitchen."

"Oh, who's getting all hoity-toity then? Got our knickers

in a twist, have we?"

Unable to maintain his indignation, Alan burst out laughing. "You're impossible."

David beamed at him. "Yes, aren't I? Always was. But you still haven't answered my question."

"I did have a brief fling with a chef not long after I came to London. He was a nice guy and taught me a lot – above all, the importance of good, fresh ingredients."

"Sounds great."

"Yeah, he was," Alan replied a little wistfully.

"What happened?"

"He went back to France. He'd been over here for a year's traineeship and went back to help in his parents' restaurant in Bordeaux. We kept in touch for a while but drifted apart. You know how it is."

"Actually I don't, Al. Know, that is. Which is rather the point, isn't it? One rather insipid marriage and a now an affair with my oldest friend. Circle of friends? Zero. Sexual experience limited to those two. Hardly qualifies me as the Casanova of Sedgethwaite, does it?"

Alan laughed, though he felt slightly uneasy at David's tone. "No, s'pose not. Still, I think you're sexy, so why worry about all the others? Much too complicated, I'd have thought."

David shook his head as if to clear it. He looked up at Alan. "I'm sorry about dragging the mood down a notch or two. I don't know why that stuff popped into my head."

"Don't worry about it, Davy. You must always – and I mean *always* – tell me what you're thinking and what you're worried about."

David grinned. "Alan?" he said. "I'm worried. About

everything." But as he spoke, his face fell; what had started out as a flippant remark suddenly turned serious. "Come to think of it, I'm not joking, either."

Alan moved and took David into his arms. "I know, Davy, I know."

David relaxed into the embrace and closed his eyes, letting out a big breath. So long as he was here, in this flat and in these arms, he felt safe. But deep down, he knew it was an illusion.

Chapter 20

Alan

"We should talk," Alan said, as he put the pasta in the pan. It was a Thursday night towards the end of May, and he and David were in the kitchen of the Clapham flat. David had arrived at his normal time and Alan had their supper all planned out.

Somehow, though, their greetings had become protracted again and they had ended up in bed. Having cleaned up and showered, Alan was now cooking their supper somewhat later than originally scheduled. "Sorry it's more pasta, by the way, but I know you like it. And this one's a bit different, made with chicken and mushrooms."

"Sound great. And yes, I agree. We should talk."

"Can I start?" asked Alan. "I thought it might help if I lay my cards on the table."

David's heart sank. *What on earth does that mean? Does he not want to see me any more?* But he spoke in a neutral tone. "Okay..."

"Don't look so worried, Davy. When we bumped into each other the day Auntie Mary died, you said that you'd made a decision. You couldn't ignore the fact that you might be bi or even gay. I told you how much I'd missed you. Remember?"

David nodded vigorously. "Oh yes, I certainly do. Remember, I mean."

"To be honest, my comment sort of slipped out – the thought wasn't fully formed until the words were out, if you know what I mean. I've been doing a lot of hard thinking ever since, particularly since you started to come and stay. I so enjoy having you here. That first night, after supper ... lying in bed holding you ... that was the best thing ever, if you know what I mean..." Alan's voice trembled slightly.

David nodded in reply. "Me too. Mind you, we've had our moments since as well."

"Absolutely. But," Alan continued, taking a deep breath, "the thing is that I've come to realise just how deep this goes. Not to put too fine a point on it, I love you, David Edgeley..."

He watched for David's reaction. David's eyes widened and moistened a little. He licked his lips nervously. "I see. Go on." He waited for Alan to continue, raising his wine glass to his lips, further betraying his nerves with a slight trembling of the hand.

"The thing is, I've also realised that I've probably loved you since we first met at junior school all those years ago. That means, if it's possible, and if you want it too, I'd quite like to spend the rest of my life with you." The last few words came out in a rush. Having got them out, Alan squeezed his eyes shut, suddenly unable to watch for David's reaction.

"Christ, Al," David replied quietly, awestruck by the

declaration. "I mean, thanks. I don't think anybody's ever said anything as nice as that to me." He looked down at the table and shook his head in disbelief. "I don't know what to say." There was a pause before he looked at Alan. "I love you too. Like you, I realise that I probably always have done – I was just too frightened to act. After all, what did we know about all this stuff?" He laughed. "I mean, two ordinary Yorkshire lads."

Alan nodded. "I know what you mean."

"I did mean what I said the other week," David continued. "About accepting everything and dealing with the consequences. When we – I – am here, everything reinforces my decision. This wonderful flat, your lifestyle, the food, the wine, even the coffee… And well … you." He shrugged. "It's that simple. I could no more go back to my old life than fly to the moon."

"Thanks, Davy. That's what I hoped you'd say."

"Mind you, I'm not saying that I've got beyond that," David added with a bark of laughter. "As I said in Sedgethwaite that day, I know what I want to do with my life but I still don't know how to get from here to there."

The buzz of the timer told Alan that the pasta was cooked. He broke off to drain it and assemble their meal. "Let's finish this after supper," he said over his shoulder.

✛

After supper, they moved upstairs to the sitting room and sat entwined together on the sofa.

"Talk to me, Davy."

"That's part of the problem, I suppose. I rather got out of

the habit of talking about my feelings, personal stuff, after you left home. There was nobody to say it to. So I shut it down."

Alan nodded. He was beginning to understand David's loneliness and fear. "Tell me how you feel and what you want to do. Then I can help."

"The first thing, I suppose, is that now I feel like a stranger in my own home."

"Why?"

"Because I don't share Mona's dreams any more."

"But that's not what's important, surely?"

"Oh, it is, I think. You see, right from when we were kids, Mona and I used to talk about our dreams for the future, about what would happen to us and our friends. About growing up and leaving the town – all sorts of things. Then, when we got married, we started to dream again – the kids, buying our own house, me getting promoted. Over the past few months, everything has changed. I realised that I didn't want to buy a house, at least not in Sedgethwaite. I don't want to stay in the town either, and I don't want to be with Mona. And now I know I want to be with you."

"I understand how you feel. I reached the same conclusions about Sedgethwaite before I came south."

"Yes, but you didn't have a wife and two children."

"No, but I was entering a completely different world, leaving everything I'd ever known behind me – including my best pal ever."

"But you were always the more adventurous one, leaving me behind to pluck up the courage to follow you."

"I wouldn't deny that, Davy. But you were always the

brightest one at school, nearly top of the class. I can't see why you stayed on the buses."

"Oh, that's easy. It was safe – paid well, no fear of failure, no challenge. But it's beginning to catch up with me now. I feel that I can't go on doing this for the rest of my life, but I'm terrified that I will."

"Anyway, this is all a bit beside the point. The main thing I was saying is that I understand a bit of how you feel."

"I know you do. Sometimes the thought of all the upheaval and the trouble it would cause to leave is just too scary. I feel so lonely up there – and that's the other problem. I realised the other day that this was the first time in my life where I can't discuss an issue with my family or friends – other than you, but you're two hundred miles away most of the time. I can't talk to Mona about this, or my mum and dad, or my brother and sister. Then I go to work and I sit in the canteen and listen to them. It's all sex, football and how many pints they managed to down last night."

"But I bet that would be the same in a London depot canteen as well. It's not a Yorkshire thing."

"True. But I've lived with it in Sedgethwaite for six years and more, and it never bothered me. Now I feel like a stranger there."

Alan tightened his grip round David's shoulders to show he understood and kissed his temple. "Go on, Davy."

"It's got even more complicated over the past few weeks. I came here to stay with you and got a glimpse of a whole other world. This flat, the food, everything … well, you know how far you've come. And for the future? You already know that I want you. But even if I couldn't have you, I'd want this life or something like it."

There was silence between them for a moment, then Alan sighed and spoke. "I get that, Davy – our feelings and your aspirations. No matter what happens over the next few weeks or months, we mustn't lose sight of them. But it's the boys, isn't it? They're the real problem."

"Hell, aye. If we hadn't had the kids, I'd be packing up and moving down tomorrow. Mona would be upset, obviously, but I think she'd survive. And besides, she'd be better off finding somebody else than sticking in a stone-cold marriage." David moved within Alan's embrace. "But number one, I can't just walk out and leave her with the two boys. And number two, I can't bear the thought of never seeing them again."

"I know, Davy. I know. It's why I wanted to have this talk tonight. I need you to know where you stand with my feelings. Now it's in your hands. We move at your pace, in your time. But what do you think could happen? Would she really try to cut you out completely?"

"I don't know, Al. Plenty of women do – hence that group Fathers for Justice. Maybe she'd allow me to see them, maybe not. It'd depend on how she felt about me – us – once she'd found out."

"Well, she certainly never approved of me," Alan responded with a laugh.

"And her mother never approved of me, neither. That'd be the problem, I think. The old bat would take great delight in painting me as a monster to anybody who'd listen."

"You should talk to your Jen. She'd be okay with all this, you know. She loves you to bits and was always very good to me."

"Do you think so? I'd not thought of that. I think you might be right."

"So think on. No need to hurry matters – but you know that might the best way to dip a toe in the water."

Veering off Course

Chapter 21

David

The sun streamed through the opened curtains. David blinked and woke up to find Alan looking down at him.

"I brought you some tea. It's time we were moving, old lad.'

"Don't I get a good morning kiss, then?"

"Of course you do. Anything to oblige," Alan replied, complying immediately.

David sat up to drink his tea. "Lovely day again," he said.

"Yeah, much too nice to work – or to wear a suit," Alan replied, as he donned his office outfit.

"Mind you, you do look sexy when you're all dressed up," David grinned.

It was mid-June; this was David's sixth overnight stay in London. They'd quickly established a pattern for their time together, usually spending quiet evenings in the flat. Alan had been working on an informal programme of gradual education about gay life, providing David with written materials – newspapers and magazines, information leaflets produced by campaign groups and a couple of novels.

David had devoured these enthusiastically and, in the process, come to realise that he was not alone. The issues that he and Alan were facing if they wanted a life together were not unique; counselling and support were available if they needed them. But making that first move was still the impossible bit. How would he get the words out?

"Time's getting on, young Davy. Time you were up," Alan said. "Especially if you want some breakfast."

David headed for the bathroom, pausing to brush Alan's lips with his own on the way, earning himself a slap on the backside for his pains. Time was indeed getting on, so neither had time to look at the paper, or read the story below the headline *Yorkshire Rail Chaos*.

The coach station was crammed when David pulled in but he managed to leave on time with a full load. The journey north was uneventful and they reached Sedgethwaite dead on time. It was there that the full effect of the lightning strike by rail crews became apparent: the queue was three-deep on the London stand, and took up nearly half the bus-station concourse. As David unloaded, three coaches from independent operators pulled in and cleared much of the queue, but there were still about forty people standing there.

He said farewell to the last of his passengers and got behind the wheel, ready to take his coach back to the depot. As he reached for the starter, Len Hedges' head appeared at the cab window. "Well, if it isn't young Edgeley," he remarked.

"Hello, Len. How's tha' doin'?"

"Fine, fine," Len replied. "Better still if I could get this

London queue shifted."

"Aye, it's bad, this rail business."

"I don't know as I'd call it bad, especially from our point of view. But I know what you mean."

"You stuck, then?"

Len nodded. "Aye. I think every coach in Yorkshire's out – and a good few from other counties as well."

"Does that mean you're looking for volunteers?"

Len grinned. "One'd do."

"Thought so. If my hours'll be okay."

"You should make it, but it might be close."

"Right. Well, this coach will want a quick clean and probably some fuel as well."

"You leave that to me, lad. Go and phone Mona and get yourself some snap."

✛

When he eventually got back to London, it was nearly eight o'clock. The traffic had been hell but forty grateful customers had made the journey worthwhile, netting him nearly half a week's wages in extra tips. After unloading, he sought advice about parking and was told to leave the vehicle where it was; the coach park was already full and, in any case, David was out of hours now and it would be illegal to drive any further.

He got out his mobile and dialled Alan's number to seek a bed for the night. To the extent that he'd been able to think ahead before setting off, he had assumed that he would be okay to sleep at the flat; indeed, the prospect of spending another night in Alan's arms had been a pretty powerful incentive for him to volunteer in the first place. It had not occurred to him that his call would go straight to voicemail or that Alan might be out.

Momentarily flummoxed, he left a message and decided to get some food. He tried again later but his call went straight to voicemail again. He decided to chance his arm and head over to Clapham. He might not know much about London yet, but at least he knew the way to Alan's place.

✤

There was no light on in the front room of Alan's top-floor flat when David got there. It was getting on for ten now, and he didn't know what he would do – go and get a hotel room somewhere, he supposed. But that might be difficult, as well as expensive.

He rang Alan's bell once more, but there was still no reply. However, the curtains moved in the ground-floor flat and a face appeared. A hand gestured towards the entrance, then the face disappeared again. A moment later, the hall light clicked on and a figure approached the front door.

David was greeted by a blond young man, about his own height, with a slim body; definitely a man, but with a touch of femininity about him. David had never come across anybody quite like him – George, the rather camp young clerk in his depot, was the nearest equivalent.

"Hello," said the young man, looking him up and down. "Were you after Alan Foreshaw? I heard his bell going."

"Yes, I was. I'm..."

"Oh, I know who you are!" the man exclaimed. "You're his hot young coach driver. Davy, isn't it?"

David was completely thrown. So far as he knew, his relationship with Alan was a secret between the two of them. He felt himself blushing.

"Sorry, that was a bit frank, wasn't it? Anyway, do come in. Alan's having a boys' night out with my other half. They should be back soon. I'm Simon, by the way."

"Oh, er ... thanks, Simon. Nice to meet you. I'm David. Al – I mean Alan, sorry – calls me Davy. It's a sort of joke, I suppose – dates back to my passion for Davy Crockett when I was little."

Simon laughed, "Wonderful! I know exactly what you mean – that *lovely* fur hat and the manly passion for his sidekick – what was he called?"

David relaxed a little. "George Russell, wasn't it?"

"So what brings you back to London so quickly? Alan said earlier that he wouldn't see you until next week."

"There's a rail strike on our route," David explained. "When I got back to Yorkshire at dinner time there was a huge queue trying to get to London, so I volunteered to help out."

"That was nice. Well done you!"

David blushed again. "Yeah, well, I thought I should do my bit, you know. Anyway, I'll get overtime and the tips were pretty good." He grinned. "Having a coachload of grateful people is a nice little earner."

"Mmm. I can imagine. Do you enjoy the job?"

"Very much," David replied. "I love dealing with the people, and I get to talk more to them on this sort of journey than on local buses. Yorkshire folk can be a bit taciturn, especially first thing in the morning," he added.

"Yeah, don't I know it? I live with one," Simon responded. "He's a real grump first thing. Come to that, he's not very cheerful most of the time," he added with a giggle.

"So what do you do for a living?"

"Ah, I'm a young man who sells antiques. I work in a shop at the unfashionable end of the Kings Road. I hope to get to the fashionable end one day."

"How did you get into antiques?"

"Lifelong passion, I suppose. I fell in love with my grandmother's Victorian and Edwardian furniture, and it all grew from there. I did a Fine Arts degree and went straight into the trade." Simon paused and then giggled again. "That's probably the only straight thing I've ever done in my life."

Initially nonplussed, David suddenly saw the joke and started to laugh. He definitely liked Simon and warmed to his sparkle. "Unlike me, who's done rather too many straight things for his own good."

"Yes, Alan rather hinted that life was a bit complicated. I do hope you manage to work it all out, because he's been a different boy since you came on the scene. When he got back from his auntie's funeral I expected him to be very sad, and he was in a way. But he had a sort of luminous quality about him – and eventually I understood why. He told me that he'd met you again."

David looked at him open-mouthed.

"Oh Gawd," Simon said hurriedly. "Have I put my foot in it *again*? My trouble is that I don't know when to shut up. Never tell me a secret unless you want it broadcast on the BBC the same night."

David laughed again. "No, no, it's no problem. It's just that... I know this'll sound daft, but I've been so busy trying to cope with my fears and feelings that I've never stopped to think about how it's affecting him."

"I can certainly understand *that*, dear boy. Coming to terms with being gay or bi or whatever can be a bit challenging at any age – but in your mid-twenties when you've already got a wife and child...'

"Two...'

"...sorry, wife and two children. It's enough to give anybody the heebie-jeebies. By comparison, I was lucky. I always knew, from at least the age of twelve, and with me there was no hiding it anyway."

"Goodness. Was that hard, Simon?"

"I'd be lying if I said it was a piece of cake, love. There was a certain amount of bullying at school – but it helped that I didn't actually care what anybody thought of me. They couldn't frighten me by threatening to out me, because I was already the one who put the 'out' in 'outrageous'. They could call me names and they could beat me up – but ultimately bullying only works if the person being bullied can be made to feel frightened. I never was. When they did beat me, I made sure that they didn't know whether they'd hurt me or not. I never reacted in front of them. Oh, I might have cried all night with the pain and humiliation when I got home – but I never let them see. Eventually bullying me ceased to be any fun. So they stopped and went and found some other poor bugger."

"Thanks – I'll try to remember that, when my turn comes."

"Oh, you'll be all right. Don't worry. Times have changed a lot in the ten years since I was at school."

"Not that much, I suspect – and certainly not in my part of Yorkshire. I shall be lucky to get out of this unscathed."

"And does that scare you so very much, David?"

"Yeah, it does. But ... but not enough to make me spend the rest of my life in my home town living a lie."

"Amen to that, love. We shall be fast friends, I can see. I shall be there, cheering you on." Simon laughed again. "And if you ask nicely, I'll even hold your coat."

"Aw, gee thanks, pal," David replied, joining in the laughter. At that point there was the sound of a key in the door and voices in the hall.

"Ah, I hear the wanderers returning," said Simon. He called out to his partner, "Peter, don't let Alan go upstairs. Bring him in – we've got a surprise for him."

As the two friends walked into the room, Peter was saying, "Oh God, he's picked up another waif and stray. Have you been out on the Common *again*, Simon?"

Simon winked at David. "No, no, I didn't need to. I found this one on the doorstep."

Alan followed Peter into the room. If David had doubted the truth of Simon's observations about Alan's feelings, he now had ample proof: Alan's face lit up and he beamed from ear to ear.

"Now there's a sight for sore eyes! Davy, what on earth are you doing here?"

David found himself wrapped in a big hug, whilst the other two looked on, smiling broadly.

Simon caught David's eye and winked at him again. "See?"

✛

"Sorry I couldn't warn you. About tonight, I mean. It was all such a rush," said David. He was tucked into Alan's side on the sofa, lights low, music playing – pretty much his favourite pastime these days. He smirked to himself. Well, second favourite, anyway.

"Didn't Mona mind? About the extra overnight?" Alan asked.

"I don't think she was best pleased – but she understood. As she said, it would do my reputation no harm either, if I'm going to make inspector in the autumn. Anyway, she'll come round quickly enough when she sees the tips I earned this afternoon."

"Do you want to be an inspector, Davy?"

David shrugged. "Not particularly, and especially not if I'm not staying."

"What would you do, then? In an ideal world, down here in London."

"Something to do with computers, I think. I used to love maths at school..."

"God, I remember that!" interrupted Alan. "You saved my bacon more than once, helping me with my homework. I was really dumb when it came to figures – still am, I suppose."

"Yeah, I remember doing your maths homework on the bus." David laughed. "Anyway, I've often thought about getting some skills in that area. I looked into doing some evening classes at one stage, but with my shift patterns and Mona and the boys, I couldn't make it work."

"Another good reason to get you out of there," remarked

Alan, kissing David on his forehead. "As I said the other day, you were always much brainier than me."

"At some things, I suppose. Anyway, you were better at the important ones – pinball and football ... and cricket. And you always had more common sense, too." David dropped his voice to a whisper, before adding, "And you're quite good at sex."

Alan threw his head back and laughed. "You always did have your priorities right, Davy. That's why I love you so much."

David reached up to give Alan a peck on the cheek. "Love you too."

"Changing the subject, what did you make of Simon?"

"I was a bit thrown at first. I've never met anybody quite that feminine before, you know? But once I'd got used to that, I really took to him."

"Yes, he's a good-hearted soul. He's been very kind to me since I moved in here."

"Yes," said David drily. "I worked out that he's some form of father confessor."

"More agony aunt – I don't somehow see Simon as very paternal."

"No, I know what you mean. But it threw me a bit when he knew about me ... us."

"Oh, I'm sorry, Davy. I never thought – I was so happy the other week that I had to tell somebody or I'd have burst. Were you very cross?"

"No, not at all. As I said, a bit thrown, no more. And it only lasted a moment. Besides, he was so sweet about it all."

"Yeah, he would be. And once he's on your side, he'll

fight like a tiger for you."

David nodded. "Yeah, I got that impression. He was telling me about school and bullying. He may not look it, but I think he's a very brave man underneath it all. I'll remember that when I need to."

Veering off Course

Chapter 22

Alan

Having received visits from David two nights in a row, the flat seemed very quiet for the rest of the week. Somehow the idea of a quiet evening at home on his own, which had seemed so attractive when he first moved in, was now losing its appeal.

Alan made himself a quick supper of scrambled eggs then prowled around the flat, remembering snippets of his conversations with David. At one point, he went into the bedroom and picked up David's pillow, sniffing it in attempt to catch a hint of his scent.

He held it to the side of his face, rubbing gently for a few moments, looking down and remembering how beautiful David had looked that morning, lying there having just woken up, hair tousled, smiling up at him as Alan brought him a cup of coffee. It was funny how it was the tender moments that always came back to his mind so vividly. Getting sentimental in his old age, perhaps.

He was woken from his reverie by a ring of his doorbell. He put the pillow back into place and headed downstairs to answer the door. It was Simon, standing there with a big grin and a bottle of wine. "As I've been deserted tonight as well, I thought we could be two lonely souls consoling each other."

"That sounds a great idea, come on in. I'll fetch some glasses and a corkscrew."

The mechanics of opening and pouring done, they settled in Alan's sitting room.

"So what's your man up to tonight?"

"Oh, dinner with Mother."

"Really? On his own?"

Simon let out a groan. "Absolutely. I simply cannot stand the woman. I never have done, from the moment I set eyes on her ten years ago." He paused before adding, "Mind you, it's entirely mutual. Peter was told, in no uncertain terms that if he must live a 'deviant lifestyle' he must do so off the premises and in strict privacy."

"You're kidding."

"Absolutely not. He is summoned for dinner about once every six months – you know, birthdays and so forth. He does the minimum necessary to keep his trust fund intact and no more. He'll be in a foul mood when he gets home, poor love. Always is."

Alan shook his head and there was a pause while he topped their glasses up.

"I loved meeting David last night, by the way," Simon said. "He's lovely, and very sweet. No wonder you've fallen for him. 'Good looking and so refined', as the song has it."

Alan laughed. "I'm glad you approve."

"Very definitely – especially because of how much he's

cheered you up over the last few weeks."

"Has it been that obvious?"

"You didn't have the sunniest of dispositions when you first moved in, darling, now did you?"

"No, suppose not."

"Quite. Anyway, you've been a different guy since David came back into your life – much more relaxed, and content with the world somehow."

Alan nodded. "I know what you mean. I have felt better – like my life has some meaning again. I was restless. I was being successful and loving the job, but it didn't mean much. What was the point of all the success? There was nobody to tell, or to spend my money on, or indulge. It seemed like an endless slog simply to watch the bank balance increase. God, I began to feel like Ebenezer Scrooge, amassing cash for the sake of it. Then Davy happened and gave me an objective in life – something to look forward to. He was a part of my life for so long when we were young, and we fitted back together like we'd always done. It felt – feels – so special, Simon." Alan was surprised to find tears welling up, whilst his own vehemence almost took his breath away.

Simon's eyes opened wide with surprise, quickly turning to amusement as he spoke. "My goodness, you have got it bad, haven't you, sweetheart? God, I hope it works out for you. He did look a bit lost at moments last night."

"Not surprising, Si. He doesn't know London very well, you're the first gay person he's ever met socially aside from me, but then he has to go home and act straight to his wife and little boys."

"We'll have to make sure that we look after him. Make

his trips down here so special that he always want to stay. Now let me see…" Simon paused, taking a swig of his wine. "Here's two ideas to be going on with: you should absolutely take him to a musical, number one. And he should meet some more gay people – your Tris, for one, and Ian. And perhaps a dinner, *chez nous*. A domestic scene with some nice respectable gays. What do you think?"

"I think they're both marvellous ideas. I'm sure he'll be terrified at the idea of meeting people, but it's the right thing to do – and the musical idea is pure genius!"

They talked some more, and the dinner was fixed for the next Friday night David had in town.

"We should have six altogether," Simon said. He paused, drumming his fingers on the side of his glass for a moment before his face lit up again. "I know, we can invite Gerry and Andrew – you know, my boss and his boyfriend. They can be a bit piss-elegant at times, but they're good people at heart. Anyway, who knows? Some of their high culture might rub off on you," he added with a giggle.

"It hasn't rubbed off on you, yet," Alan laughed.

"Cheeky bitch. I'll have you know that my culture is very high, thank you very much."

"And there's only one thing I want to rub off on at the moment, and it isn't high culture."

"Talking of things to rub off on, is David gracing us with his presence again this week?"

"Not before next Friday, no. Unfortunately, everything's back to normal on the railways."

"Oh *what* a shame. So we'll see you both next Friday. About eight?"

"Yeah, that should be fine. Davy should be here by seven

– that'll give him time to have a quick shower and change."

"Provided you don't *interfere* with him whilst he's in the shower..."

"Oh, I don't know. A quickie, perhaps..."

Simon laughed. "I forbid it! I don't want you wearing the poor boy out when he's got to be all wide awake and appreciative about my cooking all evening."

With that, he swept off down the stairs, leaving Alan roaring with laughter.

Veering off Course

Chapter 23

David

Back in Yorkshire, David found the week dragging. He did a couple of trips to London, but also had his two rest days ahead of the weekend. He could have worked one of them as overtime, which could have been useful, but life had been hectic of late so he fancied taking the time off.

However, when he awoke early on the second morning he rather regretted the fact that he was not working. The day glowered at him through the curtains and, when Mona drew them back, it was pouring with rain. That put paid to any idea of doing the garden. He volunteered to take Tommy to school and told Mona he was going to look in on his sister on the way back, explaining that it was a couple of weeks since he'd seen her.

Mona didn't get on with David's sister, though David was never quite sure why. They seemed to strike sparks off each other, and there was an unease in the room whenever they were together. By tacit agreement they rarely met; consequently David's principal contact with his siblings tended to result from his calls at their houses.

His sister Jennifer lived on the other side of Sedgethwaite in a classic 1930s' housing estate. She was a bright kid and had won a place at the local grammar school when she was eleven. A great success academically, she had gone off to university – the first in the family to do so. She'd gained a good degree, stayed on to do her teaching certificate – and promptly met the love of her life, Mark Andrews. Mark was now an HR manager in a local engineering plant, whilst Jenny stayed at home and looked after their growing family of three children and numerous cats, dogs, hamsters and guinea pigs.

"I wondered when you'd turn up," Jennifer said gruffly, when he appeared at the back door.

David beamed at her. "Aye, like the proverbial bad penny, me."

"That's not far from the truth," she replied, pulling him into a hug. Jennifer was slightly taller than David and had a generous figure, so he more or less disappeared into the folds of her dress. David, being the youngest of the three Edgeley children by some margin, had always had a special place in her heart.

"Nice to see you anyway. Mark's on holiday this week but he's out playing golf. Should be back in about an hour. Are you going to stay for lunch?"

"That would be great. I'm on a rest day, so no hurry – but I'd better be around to pick Tommy up from school. I'll stick around and say hello."

They went into the kitchen and she put the kettle on. "How are you doing, then, baby brother? Enjoying the London job?"

"Yeah, it's great. Makes a change from flogging to and

from Leeds all day and every day."

"Mum saw Len Hedges in town the other day. He said you were doing really well – you helped him out during the rail strike, he said."

David nodded. "Yes, that was fun – and the tips certainly made it worthwhile."

"Good. Apparently, Len told mum that you're staying with a friend when you're on the overnight duty."

"That's right. Alan Foreshaw. You remember him. I bumped him into him the other week when he came back for his Auntie Mary's funeral."

"Yes, I remember Alan very well. You and he were ... very close at school, weren't you?"

David looked quickly at his sister. She didn't return his stare but busied herself making the coffee. Finally, when she handed him a mug, she looked him straight in the eye. "I was always surprised you didn't go off to London with him."

"Really? You never said."

"No, well. It was your life. But why didn't you, David? Why did you stay here and marry *her*?"

Momentarily thrown by the question, David paused and once more caught his sister's eye. Realisation dawned and he sighed. "You know, don't you? About Alan and me?"

Jennifer nodded. "Before you two did, I suspect. You were *so* close – and you fitted together like a hand in a glove. Much closer than brothers. You were almost like twins." She gave a small smile. "Two sides of the same coin."

"I was frightened, Jen. Staying here with Mum and Dad seemed easier. I enjoyed my job – you know how I'd always

169

wanted to work on the buses. In any case, everything else seemed so scary. Especially being ... well, you know."

"And marrying Mona was part of the disguise?"

"Aye. Spot on. We'd always been pals right from junior school, and she seemed ... a good option. Safe, you know? It was very selfish, I realise that. You've never liked her, have you?"

Jennifer thought for a moment. "Actually, I don't think that's true. She's a very nice person and she's a very good mother. She's looked after you well enough, too. I couldn't criticise her for any of that. It's just that I never thought she was good enough for you. I know families often think that about the people their siblings marry, but this was different. When you were at school and close to Alan, you had such potential. There seemed to be so many possibilities in your life. And then I saw you run away from it all and settle for a boring job with a predictable and dull domestic life. I thought you'd do better than that – follow in my footsteps and go to college or even university. You were always the bright one at school. I couldn't help feeling that Mona was wrapped up in that decision, so I ended up resenting her."

"It wasn't her fault."

"No, I've always known that. And I used to get cross with you as well, but I suppose boys always expect to be in trouble with their big sister."

"True. But – oh, Jen, what the hell am I going to do now?"

His sister looked at him with such kindness in her eyes. "Does he still call you Davy? Alan, I mean. Like he used to."

David nodded, unable to speak, his eyes filling with tears. After a moment or two, he managed to find his voice. "I love him so much, sis, and I'm so frightened."

Jennifer rounded the kitchen table and held her kid brother whilst he sobbed, releasing some of the emotional turmoil that had surrounded him for the last few weeks. Eventually, he calmed down and she was able to release him. "Nip upstairs and wash your face, love. You'll feel better for it. It'll get you calmed down before Mark gets home."

As David disappeared upstairs, Mark came through the back door. "Was that David I saw disappearing upstairs?"

Jennifer nodded. "He's a bit upset."

"You were right, then? It is Alan?"

She beamed at her husband. "Aren't I always?" Her expression became more serious as she said, "He needs our help, Mark."

Her husband nodded. "I saw, through the window. I got home a few minutes ago but I waited till it had passed."

"He'll be better now."

David entered the room at that point and hugged his brother-in-law. He looked and felt a great deal better, the only clue to his meltdown being some redness about the eyes. "Did she tell you?" David asked.

"She didn't need to, David. I don't spend most of my life dealing with people without learning a thing or two."

"No, I suppose not." David sighed. "I don't suppose you know what I should do next, do you?"

"First of all, you need to know that we'll support you whatever you decide," Mark replied. "You're Jen's brother and we love you. All we want is for you to be happy and fulfilled."

"Thanks. That means a lot. Alan said I should come and talk to you and Jen."

"Did he now?" his sister said, a note of approval in her voice. "I always thought that lad had his head screwed on." There was a pause then she asked, "Presumably you don't want to stay with Mona?"

David shook his head. "Even if I was minded to, I don't think it would be fair to her. She deserves better. But I couldn't bear to leave the boys. If I went to London I could support them – but not to see them for months on end, to miss them growing up..." His voice started to tremble again.

"You'd need an agreement, David," Mark said. "You'd never win a custody battle with Mona, especially if you were two hundred miles away and in a gay relationship. We've come a long way in the last twenty years but not that far."

"Yeah, quite," David replied. "I don't know how she'd react... And more to the point I don't know what her mother will say. She's never liked me. I hate the thought of her bad-mouthing me to the boys and whoever else will listen for the next ten years."

"I know it's not very helpful," Jen said, "but there's only one way to find out."

"You need to go away and think a bit more," added Mark. "I should talk to Alan again. See what you both reckon. When are you seeing him again?"

"Friday night. We're going to dinner with some friends of his."

"Do give him our best," his sister instructed. "And tell

him to talk to me if he needs a shoulder to cry on. We could always give him a bed for a night or two, if it would help."

Mark added, "I've only one thing to add, though. Don't wait about too long. It doesn't take much for word to leak out or rumours to start. If Mona or her family find out from gossip rather than hearing it from you, it might make matters a great deal worse."

David nodded. "Yes, Mark, I agree," he said. "And thanks, both of you."

✛

The discussion with his sister and her husband left David in a good mood for his trip to London on the Friday. He was looking forward to the dinner at Simon and Peter's – another milestone on his road to the gay lifestyle.

He should have had plenty of time to get to Alan's, even if the M1 was much busier than usual. To his annoyance, however, the traffic came to a grinding halt as he was approaching the services at Leicester Forest East.

"Bugger," he muttered. "It would happen today of all days."

Five minutes passed, extended to ten and then ten more. Nothing moved but several ambulances and police cars passed by on the hard shoulder, lights flashing and sirens blaring. You didn't need to be much of a detective to work out that there had been an accident up ahead.

Getting moving again on their journey south would depend largely on whether the accident was after or before the next junction. If it was after, they would eventually be diverted off the motorway; if before, they were probably stuck until the police cleared the road. That could take hours.

David looked at his watch. Whatever happened, he was going to be late for the dinner party. *Shit.*

Suddenly, there was movement ahead. Brake lights illuminated as car engines were started and the traffic began to move again. David started his own engine once more and they moved off. Sure enough, the accident had occurred beyond the next junction and a diversion was in place. They had been stationery for half an hour; the slowness of the traffic, plus a diversion, would add at least another half hour to the journey – and that assumed that there were no hold-ups through central London to Victoria. That was a pretty big assumption on a Friday evening.

David had no means of warning Alan or Simon unless he stopped his coach to call or text them, which would not go down well with the punters. No, he would simply have to plough on and get in touch as soon as he could when he got to the bus station.

He reached there at seven-fifty, one and hour and twenty minutes behind schedule. At least Alan would probably not have gone downstairs yet, so he could convey David's apology and give Simon a rough estimate of when he would arrive. He felt better now that he could get in touch.

Alan picked up on the second ring. David breathed a sigh of relief when he heard his voice and started to explain what had happened.

✛

David raced across to the coach park and shut his vehicle down for the night in record time. He managed to get to Alan's at eight forty-five. Although he needed to change out of his uniform and freshen up, there was time for neither. However, he managed to be sitting in Simon and Peter's flat before nine with a drink in hand. He felt thoroughly embarrassed about being late, and apologised at least three times before Simon swatted him on the back of the head and told him to shut up and relax.

Alan was sitting next to him on the sofa and reached an arm behind him to rub circles on his back. The tension started to drain away; David melted into his lover's side, and gave him a whispered 'hello'. There was little time for any conversation as Simon whisked the first course in and called them all to the table.

The evening went with a swing with everybody busily talking, gossiping and comparing notes – everybody, that is, except David.

His five companions might as well have been speaking in a foreign language because he barely understood one word in ten. They debated the merits of somebody called Baryshni-something against another Russian bloke ... Nuritov or Nureyev. There was talk of plié, arabesque and jeté, and a whole host of other names were tossed round the table all in a sort of shorthand; the dialogue was almost impossible for the uninitiated to decipher. David heard talk of darling Sophie, Dame Marie, Madam, Darcy somebody, Anthony Dowell and so on. He had worked out that they must be talking about dance of some sort, possibly ballet, when the subject abruptly shifted.

He heard the word "conducting" at one stage, only to

realise that they were now talking about music. Then it got even more cryptic as moved into what he could only think was some sort of code.

"What do you think of the Curzon K466, Si?" Andrew asked Simon.

"You mean the seventies one with Ben conducting?"

Andrew nodded. "Sublime or what?"

"I still love the Ashkenazy," chipped in Peter. "Especially as the Curzon is coupled with K595 and Brendel is the *only* person I can bear to hear playing that."

David looked from one to the other, completely baffled. He caught Alan's eye and rolled his eyes. Alan winked, but quickly got involved as well. "I'm afraid I'm simply addicted to the music. I'm no expert. I only discovered Mozart's piano concertos a couple of years ago, thanks to my friend Tris. I don't much care who's playing them – but I can't imagine my life without them."

David smiled again at Alan and offered him a silent prayer of thanks. At least he now knew what they were talking about, even if he still didn't understand any of the words.

Soon they were off again – the new code was full of what seemed to be Italian words – Cosi, Kiri, Nozze, Barbera, Soave, some song called Non Pew Andrew – though he did dimly recognised the tune when somebody began to hum it. He laughed when Simon asked the company what their favourite Mozart opera was, and everybody chorused "the last one we saw".

Aha. Another code broken.

Throughout it all David watched the other guests, fascinated by the sharp turns in the conversation and amazed by their knowledge and enthusiasm. Alan's friends were kind and warm towards him, whilst Alan kept catching his eye, trying to offer reassurance.

If asked, though, he would have said that he was very far from coping. As the evening wore on, he came to realise the breadth and depth of his ignorance. He would be totally unsuited to a life in London; he would only hold Alan back and show him up in front of his friends. He was too thick to learn about such stuff – and not particularly interested, either. Better by far to put all this aside and stick to Sedgethwaite. Simpler, too. No complications with Mona, and he'd see his boys growing up.

The conversation took another baffling turn into a new production at the National. David wondered at first whether they were talking about the *Leyland* National – a type of bus he remembered from school days – but he caught the word Shakespeare, so assumed not. He looked pleadingly at Alan, who quickly responded.

"Sorry to break the party up, guys," he interrupted. "But young David here has to work for his living tomorrow and drive that big butch coach back to Yorkshire, so I'd better ensure that he gets his beauty sleep."

"If he needs all his strength tomorrow," Simon replied with a smirk, "you'd better make sure he gets all his oats tonight."

David felt himself blushing but Alan simply laughed. "Don't worry, Simon, I fully intend to."

They said their goodnights and David reserved a special hug for Simon. "It was a great evening. I'm only sorry that I was so late."

"Don't worry about that, sweetheart," Simon said out

loud, before dropping his voice to a whisper. "And well done. You coped amazingly well with us prissy queens tonight. Now go and look after your man."

When they got past the front door of Alan's flat, David found himself in Alan's arms, being soundly kissed.

"God, I've been waiting to do that all night," Alan said into his ear, his breath sending shivers down David's spine. "You looked so sexy when you arrived in your uniform, all flushed and tousled."

David relaxed into Alan's embrace and they stood for a few moments, foreheads together.

"I was very embarrassed to be that late," David said after a while. "What a start to my first-ever dinner party, eh? Simon was very good about it, but I bet he and Peter could have murdered me."

"Hey, don't be daft! Things like that happen all the time in London. Everybody was very sympathetic."

"Anyway, I don't suppose they'll ask me again. I must have seemed right gormless tonight. They might as well have been speaking Swahili for most of the night. It made me realise that I know fuck-all about anything."

"Not true, Davy. Granted, you might not know much about ballet or opera, but you read a lot and you're as sharp as a needle – always have been. And you loved my Mozart last week so you can't be all bad," Alan finished with a grin.

David shook his head, unappeased. "I don't know, Al. It seemed ... completely *alien*. I'm not sure I could ever belong in this world."

"You'll always belong with me, though, whatever happens – and if we don't like their world, we'll create our own, like we did before at school. Al and Davy against the world, remember?"

David nodded but beneath the surface he remained uncertain and frightened. He wished he hadn't been quite as definite about the future with his sister and her husband the other day.

Alan spoke again. "Come on, let's have a nightcap and listen to some more Mozart – maybe you'll start to understand how bloody wonderful he is." He reached for David's hand and hauled him up the stairs to the sitting room, pausing on the way to sneak a couple of quick kisses.

Veering off Course

Chapter 24

Alan

"I can't imagine not ever knowing about this music," Alan said dreamily. They had finished their nightcaps and lay entwined on Alan's sofa.

"It certainly is very beautiful. How did you come to learn about it?" David asked. "You weren't exactly an expert when you left Sedgethwaite."

"That's certainly true," Alan replied with a laugh. "The short answer is my ex-boyfriend."

"Oh, so you've had another boyfriend, have you?" David responded with mock indignation.

"Several, actually," Alan grinned, before adding, "but none to match my Davy." His face changed and he grew serious. "Not several, to tell the truth. Two short flings and one longish relationship – hardly a lot in six years."

"Tell me more."

"Tristan was the important one. We met when I was nineteen. He was two years older. He'd recently graduated from Oxford and inherited an absolute fortune from his aunt. We moved in together a few weeks later and it lasted three years in all. He changed my life." There was a pause before Alan gave a short laugh. "We still stay in touch and I've told him all about you. He wants to meet you soon."

"Christ, Al! That sounds a bit difficult."

"Trust me, it won't be. The thing that kept Tris and I together for so long was friendship, not love. Oh, true, we had some fun in bed, particularly in the very early days – but the chemistry was never really there for either of us. After a while, we both came to realise that we weren't the *one* for each other. Some day one of us would meet our life partner and when that happened we would split up. It happened for Tris two years ago; he's now with Ian, and they're both totally in love – honestly, it's wonderful to see, Davy. They were absolutely meant for each other."

David squeezed Alan's shoulder. "Do you still miss him though?"

Alan nodded. "Sometimes – especially before you came back into my life. But I mustn't complain. The three years I spent with him were such fun, and he opened my mind in ways I could not have believed possible. He took me to the theatre, to the opera, to concerts and to some amazing restaurants. Finally, Tris's farewell gift to me was the deposit on this flat."

"Al, you're kidding!"

"No. It was the only thing we ever fought over because I wouldn't accept the gift at first, but he was adamant. I'd given him three fantastic years, he said, and but for me he'd never have met Ian. That was true because Ian and I worked in the same office. We still do. In the end, I could only accept."

"Wow. Some friend."

v "Yes, he is. But, you know, his greatest gift to me wasn't the money. It was the way he opened my mind to a new lifestyle, to music, books and plays and ballets and operas – a whole world of culture that I hadn't known existed before I met him. And it has enriched my life so much, Davy. That's why I believe that we can do the same for you. I love you and I want to offer you the gift that Tris gave me."

"Bloody hell, Al. I ... er ... don't know what to say. I'm amazed. We hadn't really talked about your life down here after you left home. No wonder you've changed so much."

As if on cue, the music changed and another slow movement started. The tune captivated David; he felt his body relax. Alan watched as his face softened. They remained silent in each other's arms for the whole of the movement.

When it ended, Alan saw the tears in David's eyes and kissed them away. "That's the K467 that Simon thinks is so sublime," he said.

"It's marvellous. The tune is very beautiful. But what is it? What does K467 mean?"

"It's Mozart's twenty-first piano concerto, and we're listening to the slow movement. And it's K467, because that's the number of the work in the catalogue a man called Kirchel compiled of Mozart's complete works – hence the K."

"Thanks! Now I'm beginning to understand."

"Good. And now it's time to take you to bed. You've got that big coach to drive home tomorrow. I don't want you falling asleep at the wheel."

David grinned salaciously, before adding, "And I've got

something else to drive home tonight."

✛

The first northbound departure on David's route was later on a Saturday morning, so he and Alan were able to have a lie-in before David had to report for duty. David took the opportunity to update Alan on his visit to his sister and her husband, and to pass on their greetings and invitations both to get in touch and to stay whenever he needed to.

Alan took this as a positive step forward: coming out to anybody was a big step, a boundary crossed. That David had done that as soon as he had, and without urging, showed how brave he really was, despite his gentle, rather diffident character. It helped, of course, that Jennifer and her husband had been so supportive and understanding.

He knew how hard it was for David to cope and was determined not to push him into one decision or another. He'd decided on his role of reassurance and support, and that was what he was going to deliver; he was determined not to turn into a whiney boyfriend, always demanding affection and pushing for more. If there was one thing he was certain of in this whole sorry mess, it was that whining would drive David away very quickly indeed.

Alan returned to the empty flat after dropping David at the coach park, and it felt desolate. He drifted for a while, feeling at a loose end, but eventually roused himself and did some domestic chores. His mind kept wandering, especially when he changed the bed linen and remembered holding David in his arms the previous night. He buried his face in the sheets as he removed them from the bed, inhaling their odours.

However, he was awoken from his reverie by the ping of his mobile with a text from Tris.

TRIS:>> Hey, I'm a grass widow for the day. Fancy lunch somewhere?

ALAN:>> What's a grass widow?

TRIS:>> Ian cricketing, am on my own.

ALAN:>> Understood. Lunch sounds gr8.

TRIS:>> Pick you up in 20.

Twenty minutes later, Alan heard the throaty noise of Tris's elegant sports car in the road outside and ran downstairs to meet his old friend. Tristan greeted him with a broad grin and a kiss. "Hello there, dear boy."

"Hi. Where are we off to?"

"I thought Richmond, if that's okay. Lunch and a wander in the park. Got some news for you."

Alan laughed. "Judging by the big grin on your face, I'd say somebody might have been plighting their troth last night. Who proposed first?"

Tris laughed. "He did, damn him! Champagne and roses and a very romantic dinner. He did very well, the boy."

"And you accepted him, I trust?"

"Of course! How could I not spend the rest of my life with him?"

Alan reached across the console of the car and patted Tris's hand. "Quite right too. I'm delighted, Tris. Wonderful news. Congratulations."

"And then the bugger pisses off to play cricket!" Tris said with mock indignation. He grinned. "Still, at least I get to have lunch with my second favourite man."

Alan laughed. "How very kind. Why Richmond?"

"I don't know. It seemed right. The river, the park, maybe look at the view from the top of the Hill."

"Sounds grand. Perfect for lonely old me."

"Lonely? I thought you and Davy were going great guns! Wasn't last night the great Dinner Party?"

"Take no notice. It's all fine, really. I miss him when he's gone, that's all."

"I can understand that. It can't be easy for you both."

"It isn't," Alan responded with a sigh. "But enough of me. This isn't a consolation day out for me, it's a celebration for you! Are you going to have some form of ceremony?"

"If and when they change the law. We do want to have a party to celebrate though, but I want your Davy to be there. Do you know his schedule? Is he likely to be down on a Saturday night any time soon?"

"Two weeks' time, actually. But won't that be too soon?"

"Not at all, that would be fine. It was actually our favoured option. We want it to be fairly spontaneous, not like some bloody debutante ball, planned for months and all stuffy and formal. No, that's good. Considered yourselves invited for that Saturday night."

"Tris, that's a lovely thought. Thanks. I do so want you to meet him."

"Mmm. Me too." said Tris. "Now where are we going to eat?"

"There used to be a nice Italian near the river. I wonder if it's still there."

"Sounds ideal. A big bowl of pasta. Just the job!"

✥

The Italian was indeed still there and as good as they both remembered. The pasta was followed by *affogato*, Alan's favourite desert, and he felt content as they sipped their espresso.

"You're looking very sombre today, Alan," Tris commented. "Did last night not go well?"

"No, no, the dinner was fine and Davy enjoyed himself. He was a bit stressed, though. He was late in because there was a problem on the M1."

"Oh, no! Poor lad. What time did he arrive?"

"He got to the flat about a quarter to nine. He was a bit wound up about it."

"I'm sure he was. And how did he cope with the gay company?"

"I thought he was doing okay, but he said afterwards that it was like listening to a foreign language."

Tris laughed. "Don't tell me – with those four you had ballet, opera and Mozart, probably in that order. Right?"

Alan let out a guffaw. "How on earth did you guess?"

"I know Gerry and Andrew – bought some stuff from them. That's how I came to meet Simon and Peter."

"Of course, I understand now. Anyway, you were spot on. Poor Davy was a bit like a spectator at Wimbledon, watching those four bat back and forth. His eyes got wider and wider as the evening wore on."

"Poor dear! Did he mind?"

"I think it made him feel a complete ignoramus. I can understand it too, because it's how I used to feel – especially dining with your parents."

Tris laughed. "Yes, I remember those sessions. You looked a bit like a frightened rabbit sometimes. And yet they think the world of you, you know. Mummy always asks after you."

Alan blushed slightly. "That's nice to hear, thanks. I am very fond of them. Have you told them yet about last night?"

"Ian and I are going for lunch tomorrow for the big reveal. Why don't you come? I'm sure they'd love to see you."

"Actually, I very well might – a nice family occasion would cheer me up, I think."

Alan settled the bill – he'd insisted on it being his treat as a celebration. Tris went off to phone his mother, so their conversation was suspended. Tris was relentless when he wanted information, though: it was inevitable that the subject of Alan's state of mind and relationship with David would come up again. It did, as they stood on the top of King Henry's Mount and admired the view through the trees towards Central London.

"I'd forgotten how lovely this place is," Alan remarked.

"Not half bad," Tristan agreed. "Shame it's not clear enough to see St Paul's. And it's not as good as that pic you sent me from Sedgethwaite the other week."

"Oh, you mean the one from Town Moor?"

Tris nodded. "It looked absolutely lovely up there."

"Yes, I'd forgotten how spectacular that view was."

"How did it feel? Going back after six years."

"Very strange. That first afternoon and evening on my own, I felt completely at sea. Not my world any more. That's why I went to a hotel and not back to Auntie Mary's house. I was on home ground in a modern four-star hotel. Stupid, wasn't it?"

"No, I don't think so. You coped the best way you could. It's all we can ever do in those situations."

"True. Anyway, I bumped into Davy the next morning and the world shifted."

"Really? How come?"

"It was like finding a missing part." Alan paused and laughed, half to himself. "You know, that moment when you were a kid and you found the last Lego brick and slotted it in place. The model was complete, and you stood back to admire it."

"Yes, I know exactly, Alan. Because that's how I feel with Ian."

"I thought so. You could see it happening, even on that night when I first introduced you. It was uncanny."

"And is that how you feel when you're with David?"

"Yup. Scary, isn't it?"

"What? The fact of it, or what might happen?"

"Not the fact of it. I'm fine about my sexuality, and he's been a part of my life for so long. No, it's what might happen."

"What are you worried about?"

"Well, he's coming to terms with being bi or even gay. He's had a glimpse of a whole different lifestyle down here – which he says he wants – but he's got to confront the fact of his wife and the two boys. And he's facing that on his own, two hundred miles away from me. Why wouldn't I be worried?"

"When you put it like that…"

"See what I mean? Plus it's all so intense. He comes to me for no more than twelve hours once a week, we make love and chat a bit, I give him lots of cuddles, and off he goes again. We never get the chance to relax together, to be ourselves, wander like this in Richmond Park holding hands … you know. There's not much room for joy, Tris, and I'm terrified that it can't last if there's no joy."

"Surely there's joy in being with him, in making love?"

"Of course, and that's all new and exciting for him … and me, come to that. But if we're to build a life together, there has to be more to it. There has to be spontaneity and fun. Plus the fact that London life can seem very glamourous and exciting but, as you know, it can be absolute bloody hell too sometimes. What if he can't cope with it?"

"The rest I get, but I think worrying whether he'd like living in London or not is going a bit far, old love. Don't you? Be careful not to overthink it all."

Alan laughed. "Yes, I suppose you're right, Tris. But you can't deny that it's a bit scary – especially when there's so much riding on it, for me at least."

Tris's expression changed to one of deep concern. "How do you mean?"

Their walk had taken them to the top of Sawyer's Hill and Alan stared out at the view. The mist had cleared a little by now and he could see London's ever-changing skyline clearly.

Eventually, he spoke. "Funnily enough, I was thinking about this in Sedgethwaite the other week: somehow losing my aunt crystallised the thought. Ever since my parents were killed in that bloody air crash, I've been cast adrift and people leave me all the time. Starting with Mum and Dad, followed by my gran a few months later, and now Auntie Mary. Even you, Tris, to an extent, when you met Ian. If Davy goes as well, I don't honestly think I could cope." His eyes filled once more and threatened to overflow.

Tris moved and took him into a hug. "Hey, that's not going to happen, all right? Even if David can't get away, he'll still love you, I'm sure. And you'll have us – Simon and Peter, and Ian and me – we're your family now."

There was some harrumphing from two or three people also admiring the view at the idea of two men hugging. Tris fixed them with a haughty glare but nevertheless let Alan go. "All right now?" he asked, his voice full of concern.

Alan nodded. He couldn't trust himself to form a sentence yet but managed to say, "Thanks."

"Good. Right. Now I think we deserve some tea and a big squishy cake – and I know just the place. Come on, race you to the car. Last one buys the tea."

They made it to Tris's favourite teashop in Kensington with minutes to spare before they closed and managed to capture the last two cakes. They hadn't returned to the subject of David during the drive or over, tea but did so briefly just before they parted.

"Now, we'll see you tomorrow – usual time, twelve-thirty. Do you want a lift?"

"No, thanks, Tris, I'll be fine. I can either drive or pick up a cab."

"And on the other thing – all I can say is be patient. I agree with you about the joy thing, and I'll try to think up a way of doing that. And the only other thing is that if you need *anything*, you must call. That goes for both of us – even if it's only a chat in the middle of the night, call for Christ's sake. All right?"

Alan nodded. "Thanks, Tris. Thanks for a lovely day

and, once again, congratulations."

Tris beamed at him, before drawing him into another hug. "Thanks for my lovely lunch. See you tomorrow. And don't worry. Everything's going to turn out all right. I can feel it in my bones."

Chapter 25

David

When Alan dropped him off at the coach park, David stepped out of the car and back into his own world. After the events of the previous evening, he was more conscious than ever of the gap between them.

The contrasts occupied his mind for much of the drive back to Yorkshire. He kept coming back to the dinner party and how he had felt that the others had been speaking another language. Surely he could never be a part of that rarefied world. And, in any case, did he actually want to be?

It had all been completely alien. He wasn't sure that he really liked classical music much, not that he'd ever heard a great deal other than the stuff his mum played on the radio. But it always seemed to him that opera was all wailing and caterwauling. And ballet? Was that really for him, an ordinary bus driver from Yorkshire?

He shook his head. But he liked some of the tunes that Mum listened to, and he had certainly liked those piano concertos that Alan had played for him on Friday night.

One bit had even made him cry a little. Most pop music didn't do that to you.

He began to laugh at himself. None of that stuff was for the likes of him. It was for educated people, who'd been to a good school or university, not somebody who'd quit the education system as soon as he possibly could. He liked some of the tunes, but he didn't understand what was going on. All that talk of codas and cadenzas. What the hell were they?

On the other hand, Alan had been in the same position a few years ago but his friend Tristan had cared enough to help. He'd widened Alan's horizons and now Alan was offering to do the same for David. There was no doubt that Alan had changed and, on the whole, David thought it was for the better. He was calmer, more considered. Part of that came from maturing, he supposed. But Alan had seized whatever chances he'd been offered – and look at him now.

Was that what he wanted for himself? Or was he content with the way he was now? Well, he knew the answer to that question. Apart from anything else, he'd effectively given it to Jennifer and Mark the previous Thursday and received their blessing.

Now he had to tell Mona. But what could he say? How would he ever get the words out?

Any immediate attempt to talk to her was forestalled by the fact that she'd taken to the boys to see her mum and dad. When the opportunity arose later that evening David hesitated, telling himself that the time wasn't right and he could wait a few more days. He knew he was being a coward; he was also conscious of Mark's advice the previous week. But he told himself it was Saturday night and it was unfair to ruin their weekend. That was his justification.

Saturday night passed, and Sunday came and went too. David still couldn't think what he would say. What made matters worse was that even if he came up with a form of words, they would probably stick in his throat and he would not be able to utter them. And there would be the questions and accusations that would inevitably follow. How would he cope with those?

Once the new week started, the days flew by and he still took the line of least resistance. True, he was thinking about it, virtually all the time, in fact, coming up with possible phrases and tossing them away, as if screwing his thoughts up and throwing them into a virtual waste bin. But actually saying anything? No, not yet. He had to find the right words, wait for the right moment.

The week rolled by. Saturday came, and it was time for his next overnight trip. It was the night of Tris and Ian's party.

As with Simon and Peter's dinner party a couple of weeks earlier, the timings allowed for David to get to Alan's flat, have a quick shower and change before leaving for the party that was taking place across the river in Kensington. Just as on that Friday night, though, the vagaries of Britain's motorway system intervened.

A serious accident on the M1 closed the road at one of the places where the diversionary route was at its narrowest and most congested.

Veering off Course

Chapter 26

Alan

Alan was very keen that David should attend the party. He had already explained how important Tris was to his life and that Ian was also a very close colleague at work as well as a friend. He wanted David to meet them both.

It seemed to Alan that as many of his friends as possible should meet David and hopefully like him. He was concerned that David's lack of confidence about a future life in London should not frighten him so much that he stayed in Yorkshire. If he met and liked people, especially gay people other than Alan himself, surely a move south would seem less scary.

The other aspect was an instinctive feeling that the pair of them would need lots of support in the not-too-distant future. Alan was sure that a crisis was bound to come at some point; it would help if they had people at their backs. He knew how much Tris in particular had helped to change his own life and was sure that he could help David too.

Alan had been catching up with some work on Saturday afternoon and was about to finish when he got David's text message. He was delayed on the bloody motorway again, poor lad. Alan fired up his laptop again and called up his favourite traffic website. He immediately saw what the problem was: a multiple pile-up on the M1. The road would be closed for hours. Depending on where he was, David would either be sitting on the stretch of the road that was closed or edging his way southwards on a heavily congested diversion. Either way, there was no way that he would be on time for the party.

Alan sighed. He'd been looking forward so much to introducing David to Tris and Ian. Now, when – if – David did eventually arrive, he'd be completely knackered and stressed to hell. He paused for a moment, fingers poised over the keys, trying to decide what to do. Having assessed the options, he texted back to David.

Alan>>: Will take your party frock with me to Tris's. Grab a cab from the coach park and come straight there.

Around twenty minutes later, David gave a quick reply.

David:>> Smart thinking, Al. Wilco. Whoops, traffic moving again. CU L8R.

Alan frowned at this, but eventually translated the last bit into "see you later". He certainly hoped so. He needed his fix of Davy to get through the week.

He glanced at his watch and realised that he ought to get ready. He packed a bag for David, taking his outfit, overnight things and clean stuff for tomorrow's return northwards. Then he went into the shower and got himself ready.

With no David to wait for, he decided to head over to Tris's place in Kensington early to see if he could help. It turned out to be a wise move; the preparations were in some chaos when he arrived. The caterers had arrived late and were still setting up, and the musicians had not yet shown up at all. As a result, the house looked as if a bomb had dropped on it rather than the beautifully organised space it was supposed to be.

Ian gave Alan the job of taking Tris out into the garden and calming him down. "I'm sure it'll be all right by the time people arrive but at this moment it's best if he doesn't see what's going on or try to interfere," he said. "You've always been able to calm him down – the Tris Whisperer," he added with a grin.

Alan endured Tris's wails of frustration at the sheer incompetence of people, who, he said, were totally incapable of carrying out the simplest of instructions. And as for turning up on time, well... And so on, while they paced up and down in the garden.

Suddenly they heard a high-pitched feedback noise from the drawing room, followed by a burst of musical notes on a guitar; it was clear that the musicians had arrived. Tris's stress levels came down a couple of notches. A few moments later, a waiter emerged into the garden carrying a tray of filled champagne glasses. Tris breathed a sigh of relief. All would be well.

Then he started to panic again. "Hey, I've just realised, you came on your own, Alan. Where's David?"

Alan grimaced. "Stuck in a traffic jam near Leicester, I think. Six car pile-up and two dead, according to the web."

"Christ, Alan. Will he get here at all, do you think?"

Alan nodded. "Yeah, but I don't know what time. I brought his clothes over so that he can come straight here and change."

"Great idea, man. Did Ian sort you out a room? You might as well stay here tonight. David can go straight from here in the morning."

"Thanks, that would be great. Can I borrow a toothbrush?"

"The spare ones are still in the cupboard, old thing. Just like they used to be." Tris fixed him with a look. "Don't be a stranger, Alan."

"No, I shan't be, Tris. But this is home for you and Ian now, not me. I mustn't assume."

"Nonsense!" Tris barked. "Still yours as well, whenever you need it." He suddenly looked wistful. "I do miss you sometimes, even now. I love Ian madly but it's not comfy, like you and me."

Alan laughed but was touched by the remark nonetheless. "Hmm. That's how you think of me now, is it? Like a comfy pair of old bedroom slippers?"

Tris laughed too. "No, silly. Like a teddy bear, always there for a hug."

Alan found himself wrapped in Tris's arms, being hugged whether he liked it or not. He did, but wasn't about to admit it. Tris was Ian's now and he, Alan, had Davy. So everything would be all right, wouldn't it? His train of thought was interrupted by a loud cough. He looked up to see Ian grinning at him.

Ian winked and said to Tris, "Everybody's finished setting up. Want to check everything over?"

Tris lifted his head and blinked. "Oh, great, thanks, luvvie. You stay and cuddle my teddy bear for a minute, will you? He's all on his own tonight."

Tris disappeared towards the house. Ian beamed at Alan

and replaced Tris in Alan's embrace. "Thanks, mate. You did a beautiful job of calming him down."

"My pleasure. He wants tonight to be right, you know? Especially for you."

"I know. He doesn't seem to realise that nothing matters, provided I've got him. Now tell me about David. What's happened?"

Alan explained the delay and updated Ian on how matters stood with Davy. They stood and sipped champagne, waiting for Tris to emerge and declare everything to be ready.

After a few moments, he emerged from the kitchen door, wreathed in smiles. "All done," he announced. "Looking great." He let out another laugh. "Now all we need to make this party go with a swing is a sexy coach driver. Do you know of anybody, Alan?"

Alan was about to answer when his phone buzzed with a text. David had arrived at Marble Arch. He'd be about another hour, but at least he was safely in London.

Veering off Course

Chapter 27

David

It was almost nine o'clock when David dropped his passengers at Victoria and headed over to the coach park. He was four hours late.

He dialled Alan's number, who picked up immediately. Trouble was that David could hardly hear is voice for the music in the background. In the end, he managed to make out the words 'I'll text you' and 'I love you'. Despite his tiredness and frustration, the words made him feel warm inside.

The text reminded him to get a cab straight to the house, where he could change because Alan had taken his clothes with him. Tris's address was at the end of the message. The idea of hailing a London taxi was utterly strange. David had only used a cab on two occasions – and neither of them had been in London. He knew it was daft, but the idea made him stupidly nervous.

He headed for the main road near the coach park and saw several vehicles with their orange lights shining, indicating that they were for hire. The first two he hailed missed his tentative wave completely but when the third hove into sight he was more determined. This one stopped, prompting David to shut his eyes and swallow hard before managing to give the address to the driver. However, his voice was so tentative that the driver had to ask him to repeat it. David cleared his throat, managed to make his destination audible and clambered into the back seat. As he buckled his seat belt, he let out a sigh of relief and mopped his brow.

He was actually a paying passenger in a black London cab for the first time ever. Just like all those people on the telly. How exciting was that?

It was a typical July night in London – still warm after a day of hot sunshine and quite humid. Not a breath of air stirred the trees and there was a special quality to the sounds of the city, a slight echo that carried sound further in the thin air.

David enjoyed the breeze from the open windows as the cab crossed the Thames. They passed the museums of South Kensington and headed into the streets to the south of the Hyde Park. Rows of elegant stuccoed Victorian houses stretched in terraces on the streets they crossed at right angles. Eventually they turned left into one of them. David recognised the name from Alan's text and realised that they were nearly there. This street did not follow the grid pattern of the others, though, and bent round to the left. The cab entered a cul-de-sac and came to a halt at the end of the street.

Opposite stood a beautiful, early-nineteenth-century building with three floors. It was semi-detached house, flat-fronted. On the right-hand side, the building had a small tower, below which stood a black front door, partially open. The roof of the front porch formed a balcony, accessed from French doors in one of the first-floor reception rooms. Guests spilled out onto the balcony. The other windows were fully open. The air was full of laughter, underpinned by the buzz of conversation.

There was no mistaking the fact that there was a party in full swing; David could hear the beat of loud rock music from deeper in the house. At first he made no move to get out of the cab, spellbound by what he was looking at.

"There you are then, old son." The cab driver's voice stirred him from his reverie. "Number 48 is right over there, if I'm not mistaken."

"Oh, thanks. Sorry. I've not been before – it's much grander than I expected."

"You go and enjoy yourself, mate," said the cabbie with a grin. "Looks like a posh do."

"Thanks," David responded with a nervous grimace as he handed over the money for his fare. "Looks a bit too posh for the likes of me, though. We'll see."

The cab drew away, leaving David on the pavement opposite the house, awe-struck. Alan's building had seemed imposing enough, but this was like a small palace. He was rooted to the spot, unable to move. All those people, all elegantly dressed, whereas he was still in his crumpled and hardly fashionable coach driver's uniform. He only knew three of the guests at maximum – and even two of those were way out of his league. Come to think of it, Alan was hardly in his division these days...

If Simon and Peter were out of his league, this lot weren't even playing the same sport. He had to leave, to get away.

He did not belong here, amongst these people. He turned to walk back up the street, but at that moment the front door opened wider and a figure came down the steps. Before David could move, an elegantly dressed young man crossed the road and approached him, addressing him by name.

"David? David Edgeley?"

"Aye, that's me."

"I thought it must be. Alan said you were on the way and then I caught sight of the cab pulling up. I'm Tristram Baxter – Tris. I've heard so much about you."

Before he could move or utter a word, David found himself wrapped in a strong embrace. He was still not used to all this hugging and responded stiffly at first. Gradually the warmth of the greeting relaxed him.

"Welcome to the chaos," Tris said warmly. "Though I gather you've had some of your own tonight."

"Thanks. Yeah, just a bit," David replied. "Four hours stuck on the M1 – what a way to spend a Saturday night, eh?"

"Come away in, and let's get you showered and changed. Alan's got everything beautifully organised."

David followed Tris into the house. The hall seemed impossibly large, and there was a grand staircase leading up via a half-landing to the first floor.

At the top stood Alan with a big grin on his face. "You made it then, our Davy?" he called in his broadest Yorkshire accent.

"Aye, happen I did, lad." Relieved to see him, David grinned back and played up to the joke. "Happen I did. But I'm a bit jiggered."

"Well, get thissen oop these stairs, and we'll get thee fettled nicely."

Immediately Alan's presence made David's surroundings feel less alien.

Tris put an arm round his shoulder and gave him a squeeze. "Go on, old chap. You can relax now. No pressure. We'll see you in a while."

✦

Showered, changed and thoroughly kissed, David found himself at Alan's side in the thick of the party half an hour later. It had been a supreme act of self-discipline that the thorough kissing had not escalated into anything else, but the formal toasts for Tris and Ian's celebration were expected shortly and could on no account be missed – especially as Alan was scheduled to propose one of them.

Their first destination was the buffet. David was ravenous, having not eaten since lunchtime. The spread that greeted them looked spectacular and featured a bafflingly huge range of dishes. The sight only served to bring back with a vengeance his insecurity and sense of not belonging. He had no idea what most of the dishes laid out in front of him contained and couldn't decide what to have.

Fortunately there was a waiter there to assist, offering to add items to his plate, and naming them as they moved along. But even the waiter used words David had never heard before. Being a decidedly unadventurous eater, despite Mona's occasional attempts to tempt him with "foreign" food, David wasn't familiar with words like samosa, avocado and asparagus. Taramasalata and hummus were also mentioned but he waved them away, repulsed by their colour and texture. When offered salad, the iceberg lettuce he was used to in his burgers was replaced by leaves in funny colours and odd shapes. The waiter gave them confusing names like frisee, *lollo rosso* and rocket. Why would somebody offer him a firework in his food? And what did *oeufs mayonnaise* mean? Was it the same as hard boiled eggs with salad cream, like his mum used to make? It certainly looked a bit like that.

In the end he played safe and selected some cold meat and pink stuff, which the waiter said was salmon mousse. David had always thought that mousse came in little plastic pots from the supermarket and was flavoured with strawberry or chocolate. Finally the waiter, who was rather nice looking and seemed to have taken a bit of a shine, persuaded him to taste a little of it and bloody good it was too. That beat the tinned red stuff.

David passed on the salad, unsure whether he would like it or the oily stuff that it seemed to have been dipped in, and took a bread roll. The next trick was to eat the bloody stuff whilst also balancing a glass. Fortunately he and Alan found a table and managed to consume their meal in a fairly normal fashion.

As they finished eating, Tris appeared and dragged Alan off to do his bit with the toasts. David followed Alan from the table towards the main room but hung back near the doorway, keen to observe rather than participate, to watch what everybody else did. A passing waiter gave him another glass of wine so he was equipped for the toasts. At least he knew how that bit worked.

He leant on the door jamb, glad to take some rest after

what had seemed to be an endless journey. As he did so, he saw Simon and Peter and waved. They came over and joined him, greeting him like long-lost pals. That gave David a warm glow and made him feel marginally less ill at ease.

They stood together as the other guests assembled for the speeches. Peter was taller than David, so he masked his presence. David could not be seen by another couple who were standing nearby. But he could hear them.

"Alan Foreshaw's new squeeze looks quite hot."

David felt himself blushing.

"Oh, you mean his bit of rough?"

"What do you mean?"

"My dear, didn't you know? He's a coach driver, darling! All the way from gloomy Yorkshire, with all those moody moors! And think of those butch rubber tyres and enormous gear sticks."

"You're kidding. What on earth can Alan see in *him*?"

"Oh God knows, darling, but I can hazard a guess."

"What do you mean?"

"Think about it, love. Coach drivers – not the sharpest knives in the drawer, usually. And you know what they say."

"No, what?"

"Well, the thicker they are, the thicker they are, if you get my drift."

David blushed even more deeply and felt tears sting his eyes. Suddenly, he felt a hand in the small of his back. He glanced up and saw it was Simon. "Take no notice, hon," he whispered. "Poisonous queens." In a louder voice, he said, 'So, David, how was Yorkshire when you left this morning? Was the air a bit *thick*?"

"No actually, it were decidedly thin." David caught on and exaggerated his accent again. "It were reet chilly as I made way to t'depot. I were jiggered by t'time I got there. Mind you, I'm quite thick, so I nearly didn't make it."

Startled, the two commentators turned quickly. David and Simon stared levelly at them until they turned and hurriedly left the room.

"Serves them bloody right," Simon remarked. "Snobbish bitches. I hope that spoiled their evening and they die of shame." He giggled. "It certainly made mine. Toxic little tramps."

David laughed. He already loved Simon for his kindness on the two previous occasions they'd met. After this intervention, he was enslaved for life. But it didn't entirely remove the sting of the remarks, mainly because he felt deep down that the men were probably right. He was a bit rough and pretty thick – and certainly did not belong in circles like this.

He was only just coping with his tiredness, the stress of the whole evening from the taxi ride to the buffet, and now the bitchy but accurate remarks of Tris's guests. They had combined to ruin his mood and he had a strong desire to get out – firstly into the fresh air, and secondly away from this house, Kensington, and everything it stood for.

He left Simon's side and headed towards the front door but his progress was impeded by groups of guests waiting for the toasts. The sight of Alan brought him to a halt. He was standing next to Ian and Tris on the half-landing, about to speak. Whatever else happened, David realised that he would have to stay for this.

Alan looking so smart and handsome that David's anger and disappointment melted away. Tonight might have been stressful, nerve-wracking and hurtful, but it was still worth it because of this one man, his boyhood friend and now his lover. Again he experienced a warm glow inside, realising once again that Alan was his life from now on. No amount of fear of his lifestyle, or anger with his friends and acquaintances, would change that.

Veering off Course

Chapter 28

Alan

Alan stood next to Tris and Ian on the half-landing, shaking like a leaf. He'd spoken publicly many times at client presentations and conferences but he'd never done this sort of thing before, and for some reason he was petrified.

The audience had assembled in the large hall below and there was a buzz of anticipation. As Alan looked around and checked that everybody was ready, he sought a glimpse of David in the crowd. David seemed to be making for the front door, prompting Alan to frown and wonder what was going on.

After a moment or two, David turned and looked up, realising what was about to happen. Alan's eyes met his and they exchanged a brief smile. Alan relaxed and tapped a spoon against his glass to call for silence; fortunately people responded immediately. He closed his eyes for a moment, swallowed hard and began to speak.

"Ladies and gentlemen, it gives me great pleasure tonight to welcome you on behalf of Tris and Ian, and to propose a

213

toast to their future happiness. As you all know, legislation is making its way through Parliament this summer to allow same-sex civil partnerships from next year – not before time, I may say." This drew a ripple of applause and a good few "hear, hears" from his audience. "Tris and Ian have already made promises to each other. They tell me that they plan to use the law as soon as possible next year to make honest men of each other."

This drew more heckling from friends below, such as "about time too" and "impossible". "Don't they need an uncivil partnership?" one wag called out.

"We'll look forward very much to all that happening," Alan continued.

"Great excuse for another booze-up," somebody yelled, to more laughter.

"That's your invitation trashed, Fletcher," Alan responded, to more laughter. "Meanwhile, the chaps wanted to celebrate their resolve to join their futures together, which is why we're here tonight.

"I've known both of them for more than five years. During that time I've shared a flat with Tris and been a colleague of Ian's. I've benefited enormously from their kindness, patience and generosity of spirit, and I count myself immensely lucky to have met both of them and to be able to call them my friends. I know that you all do too." More shouts of "hear, hear". "So, I know you'll want to join me in wishing them both every happiness in their future life together. Ladies and gentlemen, I give you Tris and Ian!"

The toast was drunk and Alan's efforts duly applauded. Both Tris and Ian embraced him before they stepped forward to reply, each speaking in turn.

Alan looked for David again. He was still standing in the same spot with a gentle, almost wistful smile on his face as he listened to the speeches. He looked up once more and caught Alan's eye, mouthing "well done" up to him.

The speeches over, Alan made his way down the stairs, receiving slaps on the back and other plaudits for his efforts. He found David and immediately wrapped his arms round him. "One day, Davy. One day, that'll be us, I hope."

He felt rather than saw a nod as David clung to him.

"We've got to keeping believing that, whatever happens," Alan added.

Another nod. They separated a little, and Alan caught sight of the unshed tears in David's eyes. Alan pulled him closer, hanging on more fiercely before speaking quietly into his ear. "Come on, let's disappear upstairs. You must be exhausted, and you're driving again tomorrow."

He got another nod.

✣

"Tris said he thought you were going to run away. That's why he came out. You weren't actually going to bail on me, were you, Davy?"

They were lying together in one of Tris's spare bedrooms – Alan's old room, in fact. They were grateful for their host's invitation to stay, even if the party was still going on downstairs. It was a lot easier to sleep there than trail back to Clapham.

"Yeah, I was petrified," David replied. "For a start I'd

never been in a London taxi before – that was scary enough. But when we got here, it all seemed totally alien. All those complete strangers and their posh accents." He shook his head. "I couldn't believe it. It was all so ... *terrifying.* Not for me at all. Besides, I was still full of tension from the journey and very tired."

"Yes, I get that. Poor old Davy."

"I was just about to turn away when I caught sight of Tris coming down the steps. He was so kind. What a nice man he is."

Alan nodded, "The best."

"Mind you, I don't know what I'd have done if he hadn't come out at that moment. Wandered off into the night, I suppose... Who knows?" David suddenly grinned. "I suppose you could say that the only thing that kept me rooted to the spot was the thought of getting a cuddle from you."

"I can understand that. I am world famous for my cuddles," Alan replied modestly.

This prompted a snort from David. "Modest as ever, I see."

"Always," Alan said with a grin, before turning serious again. "Simon said something about bitchy remarks. What was that all about?"

"Oh, I'm your bit of rough, apparently. Chosen for being thick ... in all senses of the word."

"Christ, Davy, I'm sorry."

"It's not your fault. Anyway, you must admit that there's an element of truth in it. What on earth was a Yorkshire coach driver doing at a swanky place like this?"

"You're here because you're an amazing man and I love

you. I told you the other day, we make our own world, you and I. Fuck the rest of them – especially prissy snobs like those two."

"Yes, but…"

"No buts, Davy. You can hold your head up in any circle. Tris and Ian really took to you, and Peter and Simon already think the world of you. You mustn't run yourself down. In any case, it's you and me against the rest. Always has been, always will be." Alan reached across and pulled David into a full hug, then drew back to look him in the eye. "Right?"

"Right," David responded, managing to sound more certain than he felt.

Veering off Course

Chapter 29

David

Two weeks later, David's roster meant that he was in London on a Friday night again. Alan had promised to take him on a proper date the next time his overnight fell at a weekend, and this was to be the night. He had made plans to make it a special occasion, too, which entailed going to the theatre and out for supper afterwards.

Alan had sorted out the details in a couple of hurried, rather furtive phone calls to David's mobile. It was difficult, though: depending on where he was at the time of the call, David had to be careful to keep his voice neutral and his remarks formal. Alan had quickly grasped what was going on – and made some of his remarks distinctly provocative. If his aim had been to get David to blush, he certainly succeeded, especially when he told him in some detail how he proposed to spend their evening together once they got back to the flat.

The call ended in laughter as Mona came into the room having put the boys to bed. She looked at him quizzically but David avoided her eye. How did you tell the woman who was your wife and the mother of your children that you no longer loved her and wanted to go off to live with another man?

The short answer was that you didn't. At least not until you absolutely had to. He was still prevaricating and occasionally berating himself for his cowardice but, in the end, what with the distractions of work and the demands of two lively little boys, there wasn't much room in either of their lives for existential conversations or discussions about relationships.

Friday duly arrived and David left home shortly after lunch to report for duty. When he pulled onto the stand in the bus station he had a bit of a shock for there, at the head of the queue, was Douggie Thorpe, the depot's union chairman. He and David had not been on the best of terms since the row over driver selection for the London contract a couple of months earlier. He seemed friendly enough today, though.

Douggie explained that he and his wife were going down to London for a weekend to see his wife's sister. "She wants to see some bloody musical or other," he moaned to David, "so I had to bring her in the end."

The journey south was uneventful. The motorway was busy but the fact that it was Saturday meant fewer lorries, so the roads seemed that bit more spacious. David pulled into the Victoria terminal dead on time and dropped everyone off. Douggie and his wife thanked him for a good run. David, in turn, wished them a pleasant weekend.

Having parked up, he made his way to Alan's. There was no time tonight for an extended hello kiss as they had to be ready and back into Central London for curtain up.

David had been looking forward to this all week. His only other experience of the theatre had been an annual visit to the pantomime with the local scout group – accompanied by Alan, funnily enough. He remembered enough about those visits to know that he liked live theatre a lot, so this was going to be great.

The show was *The Producers*, Mel Brooks' stage musical adaptation of his own film. As boys, David and Alan had loved the original film, counting it – alongside the same man's spoof western *Blazing Saddles* – as one of the funniest comedies they'd ever seen.

Simply sitting in the Theatre Royal in Drury Lane was a treat; even though the auditorium seated some 2,000 people, the atmosphere was intimate and warm. David's excitement was palpable as he looked around. He could barely sit still and felt a strong need to have some physical contact with Alan all the time – thighs or calves together, hand on arm or shoulder to shoulder, it didn't matter as long as there was a connection. It was as if he needed to prove to himself that he was awake and not dreaming it all.

As the overture began and the lights went down, he reached for Alan's hand and held on to it with an almost vice-like grip for the rest of the first half. When the show's first big number began, David felt his jaw drop and the hairs on the back of his neck rise. Tears sprang to his eyes. He was at his first ever West End musical, and he was totally hooked within the first two minutes.

✤

"No need to ask whether you enjoyed that," Alan said,

as he returned, beaming, from the bar with their drinks.

They were standing in one of the most famous gay pubs in London's West End. David had been admiring the extravagant etched-glass decorations whilst Alan was at the bar – not to mention gawping at some of the more extravagant clientele.

David could not stop smiling. "Fantastic. Magical. Hilarious. What can I say? I loved every minute. Thank you so much for bringing me."

"My pleasure, Davy. I don't think I've ever seen you look as happy as you did in there tonight. Talk about stage struck." Alan shot him an affectionate look before glancing at his watch. "Peter and Simon should be here any minute then we can go and have some supper. I don't know about you, but I'm starving."

"Yeah, it's a long time since my sausage roll at Leicester Services."

Peter and Simon walked into the pub at that moment. They had been to a different show and Alan had arranged to meet them for supper. As a special treat, he had booked the four of them into The Ivy, one of London's most famous theatrical restaurants.

After hugs all round, Peter and Simon declined a drink in the interests of getting to the food more quickly, so they moved towards the pub exit. Alan and David were holding hands. Simon moved closer to David and put his arm round his waist. "And how's my favourite coach driver, then?"

"Bloody great," David responded. As they crossed the threshold onto the pavement, he leant in and kissed Simon on the cheek. "The show was fantastic. I was blown away!"

"Oh, I am so glad. Alan's been on tenterhooks all week

in case you absolutely hated it."

David turned from Simon, intending to speak to Alan, but what he saw on the pavement in front of him brought him to a sudden and complete standstill. For there, with a look of utter disgust on his face, stood Douggie Thorpe. As he recognised David, his expression changed to a half smile. But the eyes gleamed with malice.

"Bet your Mona'll be interested to hear about this," he said with a sneer. "Fucking queer. I hate you lot." He turned on his heel and walked off in the opposite direction, dragging his confused wife behind him.

"Oh shit. That's torn it," David said looking at his three friends.

"Who...?" began Alan.

"That was Douggie Thorpe, the union chairman. At the depot, I mean. He'll bloody love this."

"Oh fuck."

"Yeah, you might well say that. The shit will really hit the fan now."

✛

"He might not tell anybody, Davy."

"And pigs might fly. Come off it, Al. Did you not see the look on his face?"

They were back at the Clapham flat, sitting on the sofa. David was bolt upright, his body rigid with fear. Alan rubbed his forearm gently to try to ease his tension. They had continued with the visit to The Ivy and enjoyed their meal – but the sight of Douggie Thorpe and his hostile reaction had robbed the evening of its magic. David had found it difficult to respond cheerfully to the other three. The joy he had felt during and after the show had been taken from him, as if fate had switched the light off and plunged him into the darkest of moods. It had been a cruel blow, the sight of that one man and the evident malice in his reaction.

"It's my own fault. I've been putting off telling Mona for weeks – I couldn't think what to say. In any case, I was sure I'd never get the words out. I dithered about and now look what a mess I've landed myself in. Fucking idiot, I am."

"You mustn't blame yourself, Davy," Alan responded quickly, moving closer to him and putting an arm round his shoulder. "I keep telling you, it's bloody difficult stuff all this. I'm not surprised you couldn't find the words."

David felt some of the tension leave his body as he relaxed into Alan's embrace. When he spoke again, there was a note of resignation in his voice. "No, well... The damage is done now." He let out a short bark of laughter. "I suppose it'll save me having to find the words."

"I suppose you could always ring her. Try to soften the blow," Alan mused, but David shook his head.

"I couldn't tell her over the phone, Al."

"No, I suppose not. Except that at least she'd find out from you – not local gossip."

"We're back to finding the words, though, Al. How do you say it? Christ!" Suddenly, David collapsed like a tissue plunged into water. His hands came up to his face, and he began to sob.

Alan reached round and drew him into a hug, trying to offer comfort and to reduce his pain. David immediately felt a little better. As the moments passed, his sobs subsided and he calmed down.

He sat up, wiped his eyes and blew his nose. "I'm sorry, Al. I didn't mean to upset you. I just … you know."

Alan nodded. "I do, old son. I do. I wish there was something I could say or do that would make it better."

Another thought struck David, and he carried on as if Alan hadn't spoken. "And what about Mum and Dad? Christ, I'll bet somebody will pass it on to them as quick as Mona. Oh, fuck!"

"You could always ring Jen. About your mum and dad, I mean."

David brightened. "Aye, I could that." He reached for his phone but quickly realised the time. "But not at half past one in the morning."

Alan tightened his grip on David's shoulders. "Come on, then, it's time we tried to get some sleep. You've got a coach to drive home tomorrow and all this lot to face. I only wish I could come with you."

"Not home, Al. I'm not going home, only back to Yorkshire. My home's with you now."

Veering off Course

Chapter 30

Alan

They awoke simultaneously the following morning in response to Alan's bedside alarm. Rather to their surprise, they had both fallen asleep virtually straight away the previous night and had slept through. Now, as they lay still, wrapped in each other's arms, they came to terms with the start of the new day. Inevitably, the import of last night's events broke into their consciousness once more.

Alan could feel David's body tense in his embrace but when he looked at his facial expression, the fear and worry that he had seen the previous night had disappeared. It had been replaced by a look of fierce determination. "Are you okay?" he asked.

David nodded. "Just before I went to sleep, I suddenly realised that this here – what we have together – is what matters now. I can't stop all the other shit – that's going to happen whatever. I've got to get through this, but I can do it knowing you're here for me. And we've got the rest of our lives together." He moved from Alan's embrace, got up quickly and grabbed his mobile. "Time to start. Need to talk to Jen sooner rather than later, I think."

Alan lay back in bed, full of admiration for the grim resolve on David's face as he speed-dialled his sister. The next few days were going to be bloody difficult, but he was sure that David would be able to cope in the end.

The phone at the other end was obviously picked up quickly. "Jen? It's David. Sorry it's so early, but I've got a problem...'

David wandered from the room so Alan could not hear the rest of what he told Jennifer, but he could hazard a pretty good guess. Jennifer and Alan had never been close as youngsters, but she had tolerated him as her brother's pal. Alan had always known that she was intensely loyal to her siblings and fiercely protective of David. She would be critical of David's hesitation in telling his wife and his parents about his sexuality, a hesitation that could only make this new situation infinitely worse, but he was confident that ultimately she would understand and help as much as she could. Alan did not know her husband Mark at all but, from all David had said, he sounded like a good guy. And he knew his stuff on the HR side. That might come in very useful.

Alan lay back on the bed, hearing the rumble of David's voice. Meanwhile, he replayed David's words from the previous night. "My home's with you now." Even now, twelve hours later, Alan felt the impact of those words. At the time, he had swallowed hard and looked his old school friend in the eye. "Christ, Davy. That's a bloody wonderful thing to say. Are you sure?"

"Yeah, I'm sure. I mean it. You're stuck with me now good and proper, Alan Foreshaw. You might as well get used to it. Especially since, after tomorrow, I may not have much of a choice."

Whatever happened today and over the next few days, Alan would remember those words and take comfort from them. He feared he was going to need it.

Eventually, David's conversation came to an end and he reappeared in the bedroom, looking surprisingly bright. "She's going round to Mum and Dad's straight away. She wasn't best pleased with me for havering about, but she understood why. She says Mum and Dad will be upset but will probably come round – they've suspected for years, apparently, and were always fond of you. But they'll be frantic about the boys, and the thought that they might never see them again."

"God, I can well understand that. Imagine being kept from your own grandchildren."

"Quite. Jen says she'll try to talk to Mona before I get home but she's not confident that Mona will even take the call."

"I can understand that too, I suppose."

"So can I, Al. So can I." Suddenly David started to fold again. He ran his fingers through his hair, and fear and trepidation appeared on his face. "Christ, Al. What now?"

"You do what you have to do, Davy. Go and drive that coach of yours back to Yorkshire. Be the professional you are and afterwards face the music – whatever tune they're playing. Remember that I'm only a phone call away."

Not for the first time in the last fourteen hours, Alan cursed the week-long course he was booked into, which started the following night. But for that, no power on earth would have kept him away from Sedgethwaite and

David's side.

✛

When Alan got back to the flat after dropping off David, he made some more coffee and sat in the kitchen trying to read the Saturday paper. He found it impossible to concentrate on any of the stories; his eyes went out of focus after two paragraphs of an article and a few minutes later he found himself staring into space, having constructed yet another scenario for what might happen and then worrying about it.

After a couple of hours he gave up and went upstairs to tidy up. There was the bed to make and last night's glasses to clear away. The bathroom was in a bit of a mess too after they had showered hurriedly that morning.

Alan had entered into his latest idle speculation when the doorbell jerked him out of his reverie. He groaned but moved to answer it.

Simon came bustling into the flat and made himself comfortable in the kitchen. "You got him away all right, then?"

"Yep, but he didn't want to go."

"Not surprised, poor love. I can't even begin to imagine what sort of shit storm he's going into."

"Me neither, Si. Still, he managed to speak to his sister this morning and she's gone round to see his mum and dad. She also promised to try and talk to Mona, but they don't get on very well, apparently."

"Oh, families," Simon said with a snort. "Don't you just love them?"

"Don't know. Haven't got one any more."

"Oh, Alan, I'm sorry. That was very insensitive of me. Do forgive me."

"No, you're all right, Si. Don't worry, it's fine. It doesn't worry me most of the time, but every now and again I get caught on the raw."

"Yeah, I understand what you mean. Anyway, David's talked to his sister. What now, do you think?"

"Gawd knows. I just wish I could be there for him – at least somewhere nearby – in the area, if not right by his side. But I've got this bloody course for three days from Monday, and my boss would kill me if I pulled out."

"Don't worry, we're around all week so let us know if David needs anything, or if he needs to come here. Tell him to get in touch. I made sure he got my mobile number the other week."

"Thanks. That's very kind, old love."

Simon suddenly snorted with laughter. "I suppose if there's any consolation, at least it'll bring matters to a head one way or another."

"Yeah, but which way, Si? What if Mona forces him to choose – me or the boys? I might never see him again!"

"Oh, hush. It's not going to be like that at all. David's in much too deep to abandon you, love."

"He did tell me last night that this was now his home, I suppose."

Simon beamed with triumph. "There you are! Told you he was a keeper the other week. But seriously, Alan. David loves you, and he's not going to give up on you."

Alan rubbed his hands over his face and then looked up. "God, Simon. I hope you're right."

"I'm always right, darling. Didn't you know?" He giggled. "That's what Peter loves about me!"

"Oh, sure," Alan replied, with a laugh. He realised that it was the first time he'd laughed today, and he silently blessed Simon for it.

"Right, now. Off you pop and get dressed up to look fabulous. We're taking you out to lunch."

"Si, there really is no need..."

"Nonsense. You can't sit here moping about and worrying all day. Come on, best bib and tucker, darling. We're lunching at The Savoy."

Alan laughed again. "Oh, well. In that case..."

Chapter 31

David

Alan had driven David to the coach park in plenty of time for him to get his vehicle ready. David found it extremely difficult to leave him. After they arrived at the entrance, they sat in the car for a few minutes, holding hands tightly without speaking. Eventually, David straightened his back, gave Alan a slightly tearful smile, got out of the car and stepped back into his other world.

His first worry was whether Douggie Thorpe was travelling home on his coach but he quickly remembered that Douggie and his wife were staying in London tonight and travelling home tomorrow. That was a relief. It might also mean that the process of spreading the word would be delayed for twenty-four hours. That would certainly be a bonus.

He pulled on to the stand at Victoria and scanned the queue. There was no sign of Douggie. He breathed a sigh of relief and set about his duties.

Even without a full quota of lorries, Saturday afternoon traffic on the M1 was heavy and progress was delayed further by a sudden downpour near Leicester. Thus, they were a few minutes behind schedule when David pulled into the bus station in his home town shortly before six-thirty.

Having dropped off his passengers, he set off for the depot. He would have a few more minutes' respite before setting off for home, fuelling his coach and putting it through the wash before parking it up for the night,

The town centre was quiet as he passed through; shops had closed before teatime, whilst the pubs and bars were starting to open and preparing for night to come. They were still quiet at the moment but would be busy later, full of Saturday-night revellers.

For the time being, the sound of David's vehicle echoed through the empty streets. His eye caught familiar landmarks – the medieval parish church, the Victorian town hall, the art-deco flamboyance of the Odeon cinema. Then there were the distinctive outlines of familiar shops he had known since childhood like Woolworths, British Home Stores, Marks & Spencer, and Winkworth & Tattersall, once the local grocers and now an upmarket delicatessen. Not that the likes of his family had ever gone into a posh place like that.

Was he really about to say goodbye to all this? Completely disrupt the settled pattern of his twenty-five years of life? Part of him could not help being terrified at the thought. He would be leaving so much behind – much that felt familiar and safe. But he had been chafing against familiar and safe for months now. Surely the prospect of a new life in London with Alan was much better.

That was what he had to believe in order to sustain himself

through the ordeal that he now faced. His new life would be exciting and challenging – but he'd have the love and support of somebody he'd known since the age of nine. It would be all right. He was going to be fine. Nevertheless, he swallowed hard as he turned into the depot, wondering whether any gossip had preceded him and, if so, what sort of reception he would get.

As he walked into the office to sign off and hand in his ticketing gear, he bumped into Jack Davis, the depot inspector, who was about to finish for the day. He nodded. "Evening, Jack."

"Ah, David. I was hoping to see you before I left. Pop in here a second, will you?" Jack indicated a small ante-room by the entrance to the main office.

David did as he was asked but his heart was thumping in his chest. He remained standing and blinked nervously as Jack started to speak.

"I wanted to warn you. I know you got across Douggie Thorpe during that row over the London service back in April, didn't you?"

"Yes, I did."

"He's now getting his revenge, as he usually does when people cross him. I gather you bumped into him in London last night?"

David shut his eyes, knowing what was coming next. His throat was constricted, so he couldn't speak. He nodded.

Jack shook his head. "What were the odds on that, I wonder? Anyway, the point is that he's already been on the phone, spreading it around. From what I can gather, all the members of the committee know, and it's going from there."

"Oh, Christ."

"Don't get me wrong – whatever happens in your personal life is your own business, provided it stays out of this depot. But I wanted you to know what's being said. Not only about you being ... about who you were with, but also about going behind Mona's back. For some reason there's some people here with some pretty strong views on that subject, and life may get a bit difficult."

David took a deep breath and braced himself once more, as he had done first thing that morning with Alan. "Thanks for the heads up, Jack. Can't say I'm surprised. I thought he'd move quickly. A good juicy bit of gossip like that – I bet he couldn't wait."

"Are you going to be all right?"

David gave a short bark of laughter. "I'll let you know. Seriously, it's my own fault – I've been havering about this lot for weeks. I could have done with choosing my own time but, other than that, it had to happen."

"Should I look to cover your shifts next week?"

"I think you'd better, Jack. One way or another, I may not be here to work them."

"Right you are. You'd better go and face the music, lad."

"Yes, I had, hadn't I?"

"All the best, David."

Chapter 32

Alan

Simon, Peter and Alan enjoyed a long, relaxed and boozy lunch and eventually rolled home around five-thirty. His friends had generally done a good job in distracting Alan, stopping him from worrying when there was absolutely nothing he could do. David had to get back to Yorkshire and finish his duty before he would find out what consequences would flow from the previous night's events.

Simon and Peter were going to a concert that evening, leaving Alan to his own devices. In theory, he welcomed some peace and quiet so he could relax and get his thoughts in order. But it quickly became clear that the practice was rather different, and that the last thing he would be doing tonight was relaxing, at least until he knew David was safe and out of harm's way.

He took a long bath, and certainly the hot water and some special bath salts succeeded in soaking away much of the tension from his muscles. But any attempt to get his thoughts into any sort of order was completely futile.

His mind resembled a kaleidoscope – a continually shifting pattern of thoughts, worries and imagined scenes. In some, David confronted his enemies successfully. Others ended less well, with abuse of one sort or another, either physical or verbal. He pictured David at his parents' house, prompting a flood of childhood memories. Alan could picture the rooms of the house quite vividly. What would happen there? A stern, unbending father deaf to the pleas of a loving mother, perhaps? David's father was certainly capable of being stern, as the two boys had had occasion to discover in the past. Equally, he could be kind and very gentle. David's mother, on the other hand, had always demanded the highest standards of behaviour from her children, and she could be very strict, especially if she thought that those standards of behaviour or manners were slipping. Quite how leaving a wife and children to go and live with a man would play on her scale of gentlemanly behaviour he didn't know, but he guessed it would not be high.

As he got out of the bath, he heard the ping of the text notification on his phone. He grabbed for it and it almost slipped through his wet fingers, but he managed to prevent himself from dropping it.

DAVID:>> Just got back to the depot. Gossip about last night spreading quick. Now heading home.

Alan groaned. The poor lad! What now? He dried his hands and typed a quick reply.

ALAN:>> Inevitable, I suppose. Still bad news, tho. Go carefully. Love you.

DAVID:>> Will do. Will keep you informed. Luv U2.

Alan dressed and returned to his kitchen. He ought to think about supper, he supposed, but he was not very hungry after his generous lunch. He stared gloomily out of his window across the Common. It was starting to get dark and the lamps that illuminated the paths were just coming on, bathing those people walking across it in a blue-grey light.

He loved the view from his kitchen; it had been one of the things that had sold him the flat in the first place. He and David had stood here only last night, joking about all the adventures that might be happening out there somewhere. The cruising areas on the Common were famous; Alan had been forced to admit to visiting them himself several times when he first came to London. He had never been successful, though, being much too naïve and nervous to succeed in hooking up with someone.

He recalled the banter with pleasure, only coming back to earth when his phone pinged with another message.

DAVID:>> Home now. About to go inside. God. Am frightened, Al! Luv Davy.

ALAN:>> Stick to your guns. Remember always that I love you. Good luck.

Veering off Course

Chapter 33

David

David felt slightly more relaxed as he went up the path to his front door, grateful for the contact, however brief and unsatisfactory, with Alan. He was unsure what sort of reception he would get; that would depend on what stories had reached his wife and from whom. Even if she had heard nothing yet, he knew he would have to come clean tonight. He could start by telling Mona about his relationship with Alan. It seemed to him that this was the best way to begin – to introduce the subject and gauge her reaction before deciding how to proceed.

The first thing he noticed when he got through the front door was how quiet everything was. No boys. That was a bad sign.

He walked into the kitchen, but that too was quiet. No signs of preparation for any supper for him, either. Another bad sign.

"Mona? I'm home. Where are you?"

"We're in the front room."

Odd – that isn't Mona's voice. It's her mother's. Oh Christ!

Faced with the fact of his mother-in-law's presence, he realised that it was probably inevitable. It just hadn't occurred to him that she'd be there.

He could have cut the atmosphere with a knife when he walked into the front room. Both women were sitting on the sofa, hands in their laps, mouths tightly shut with only the thinnest line of lip showing. He met Mona's eyes; they were cold and unforgiving.

"Where are the boys?"

"They're staying with my mum and dad tonight. Dad's looking after them at the moment," his wife said flatly. "I thought it would be best as we have to talk."

"I suppose you're right."

To David's intense relief, his mother-in-law rose to leave. "Right, Mona, now that he's home I'll leave you to it. Ring if you need me." She walked to the sitting-room door, acknowledging David with a curt nod before turning back towards her daughter. "Goodnight, love."

"Goodnight, Mum."

Her mother closed the front door behind her.

"Tea?" his wife asked.

They moved into their narrow galley kitchen and Mona went to the sink. She filled the kettle and switched it on. David remained by the door, unsure of what to do or where to stand. Mona stayed by the sink. The silence between them lasted until she had made a pot of tea. David stood at the other end of the work surface, near the door to the hall, and watched her.

Once the tea had brewed, she turned to face him and folded her arms. "What's going on, David? What happened last night?"

"I was leaving a pub in the West End with Alan and two of his friends – I kissed one of them on the cheek at the moment Douggie Thorpe was walking past."

"And that's all?"

"That's exactly what happened. Douggie made some remark about telling you and hating queers and stalked off. I take it he did tell you?"

Mona let out a bitter laugh. "Oh yes, he couldn't wait. He was on the phone this morning before nine. Thought I ought to know that my husband was a queer, et cetera, et cetera."

David nodded. "I assumed he would."

"So, are you?"

"What?"

"What he said. Are you gay?"

He nodded. "Probably. At the very least bisexual."

"And are you in a relationship with Alan Foreshaw?"

David nodded again. "Yes, I am."

There it was. Out there. He'd managed to utter the words.

"Oh. My. God," Mona responded, drawing out each word. There was a pause for a few seconds. Suddenly, she let out a short laugh. "Well, that answers a few questions, I suppose."

There was another pause while she poured two mugs of tea and moved one along the worktop towards him. He thanked her.

"No, thank *you*, David Edgeley. For nothing. For lying to me and cheating on me for the last six years." Her voice was rising in pitch, her tone becoming steadily more angry.

"No! Mona, No! It wasn't like that at all. Please believe

me."

"Oh, come off it! Do you mean to tell me that you didn't *know*, when you married me? That you were queer? You stood in that church and told *lies* so that I could be your cover story, didn't you?"

David buried his face in his hands for a moment. Of all the scenarios he'd played out in his mind over the last few days, this hadn't been one of them. The anger in his wife's voice was obvious and expected, but he hadn't expected the hurt. He had never thought of himself as having lied to her – at least not until Alan had come back into his life three months ago.

He lifted his head from his hands and met his wife's eyes. They were full of tears and pain. She held his gaze for a moment and then turned away.

"I swear I didn't know when I married you, Mona. You have to believe me. Alan and I had fooled about once, on the night before he left for London, but that was months before you and I got married. I didn't see him or exchange one single word with him from the day he left until a few weeks ago, until that morning when he got on my bus in Leeds. And there was certainly nobody else. It was just... Seeing him again brought it all back. How close we'd been as boys, how I'd missed him when he first went off to London. I'm sorry."

"Sorry? You're *sorry*? Is that to be my consolation for wasting six bloody years of my life? Led down the aisle so that you could have cover? So that you could prove that you were a man?"

"Mona, I..."

"Don't you Mona me, David Edgeley. How could you?

How could you pretend you loved me when all you were doing was dreaming of Alan bloody Foreshaw?"

"But it wasn't like that! I did – do – love you. We've had some good times together and you've been a good wife to me, Mona. Never think otherwise, please."

She scrunched her face up and wriggled with distaste, curling her lip. "It makes me feel dirty. Thinking of all the times we made love, that you didn't really want me at all. Now I come to think of it, I suppose that was why you didn't want to do it often, wasn't it?"

David shook his head. "It wasn't like that, Mona. Please stop saying things like that."

"Are you really telling me that you enjoyed it, then, David? Because I don't bloody believe you. Can you stand there and tell me that you didn't think of him when you were with me?"

He wanted to lie, to tell her that it wasn't true. But he knew it was, particularly lately, and he stammered slightly and blushed, muttering, "Only since I saw him again."

"Have you any idea how that makes me feel, David? After all this time? I was nothing more than some sort of substitute for the *man* you actually wanted."

"But that isn't true either. I didn't use you. I really did love you, Mona. I still do. You've been part of my *life* since the infants' school, and I would never willingly hurt you. We've never been less than very close friends and we still could be, if..."

"Friends? You want to be friends?" Mona let out a sarcastic laugh. "And a fine friend you turned out to be, didn't you, David? Lying and cheating for six bloody years, pretending to be something you're not. Like a real man!" She almost spat the last two words before resuming. "Friends! That's absolutely priceless! You want to cast me aside for that – that queer bastard and you expect to stay *friends*?"

"Look, I made a mistake. I'm sorry, Mona – and there's nothing you can say, no insult you can throw at me, that I haven't thrown at myself over the last few weeks. If I'd known, if I'd done it all deliberately to lie about myself, then you'd be right. But I promise it wasn't like that. I honestly loved you and really did mean all the 'till death do us part' stuff. Please believe that, 'cos I did not lie to you. As I said, you've been a good wife to me and you make a bloody marvellous mum..."

Even hinting at the existence of the boys was a total mistake. "Yes, and that's another thing, isn't it? I dare say you'll be up and off to your fancy boyfriend in London, leaving me here with the kids. Kind of you to give me ten or fifteen years of struggling to bring them up as a single mother."

"I promise you it won't be like that. I haven't said I'm leaving, have I? And even if I do, or you throw me out, I promise that you won't be any worse off than if I'd stayed. And I want to be around to help support you."

"Generous of you, I'm sure. But you needn't think it's going to be like that. Oh, yes, you'll pay – I'll make sure that you do, and if needs be I'll drag you through every court in the land to make that stick. But you needn't think that you'll see those boys ever again once you walk through that door. I'm not having my children exposed to a pervert like you."

It was like watching a slow-motion car crash. He could

see how Mona's hurt was morphing into a deep, burning anger fed by bitterness and evident disgust. He had not bargained for that – and he knew who had to thank for it, too. Dear Cheryl.

"I don't think you really mean that, love."

"Don't 'love' me, David. I am clearly not your love and never have been."

"Stop saying that! It's not true! I'll say it again. I never lied about my feelings towards you – and I was, and am, very proud of our children and how you look after them."

"You've got a bloody funny way of showing it, that's all I can say."

"What do you want me to say? That it's all some ghastly mistake? That we should pretend this never happened and get on with the rest of our lives? Because that would be living a total lie, wouldn't it? Staying together for the next fifteen or twenty years, purely to keep up appearances? Is that what you want?"

He paused, hoping that his words would sink in. "Can you imagine that, Mona? Smiling for our parents and pretending that everything's wonderful when it isn't? And they know it isn't. Is that what you want? Lying consistently and steadily to everybody – including the boys – for the rest of our lives? Ruining our whole future for one mistake six years ago?"

"And what is *my* future to be then, David? A single mother stuck in a corporation house on Beckett's Hill, I suppose. What about that house we were going to buy together in the autumn? What about all our hopes and dreams for a better future for us and the boys? You were going to get made up to inspector and we could have had a nice life – giving our boys a better chance in life than we ever had. Not much chance of that now, is there? They'll be another pair of fatherless teenagers on a council estate with no future and no hope of one. God, I hate you for this, what you're doing to me, to them."

"It needn't be like that."

"Oh, and how are you going to stop it, eh? How's little Tommy going to feel when I tell him that his daddy's never coming home again? Tell him what his daddy does in bed with another man? Because as sure as hell if I don't tell him, some bully at school will. Will Kevin even remember you at all? I doubt it – all he'll ever know is the gap he'll have had in his life – the gap his daddy should have filled."

David felt his eyes filling with tears. He wanted to reach out to her but couldn't. He wanted to prove to her that it wouldn't all turn out like that, but he knew deep in his heart that it very probably would. His arms went out and he took a step towards, her but she immediately took a step backwards to maintain the distance between them. His arms fell to his sides and he resumed his position by the door into the hall.

"Mona, I promise that I will do my very best to prevent that from happening. If you let me, I'll be around for the boys as much as I possibly can be. It's been the thought of leaving them that's made me so miserable over this."

Mona laughed sarcastically. "Nice of you to reveal the truth, David. You don't actually care a fig about what happens to *me*, do you? As long as the boys are all right. Typical bloody man."

"Stop saying things like that!" David allowed his frustration at the way the conversation was going to take over for a moment, raising his voice and speaking through a clenched jaw.

"Yeah, that's it. You can be a proper man when it suits you. I'm not doing what you want, so you get aggressive."

Realising the grain of truth in Mona's words, David took a couple of deep breaths and tried to calm himself down. "Mona, please believe me when I say that I didn't want any of this to happen. I can't help the way I was made, and I didn't ask to fall for Alan – but I have. I didn't decide to act on those feelings lightly, or without thinking of the consequences for you and the boys. I genuinely didn't know about this when I asked you to marry me, and I am genuinely sorry that I've hurt you so much. I still love you, but not in the way you wanted or expected. I don't want to desert you or the boys, but obviously if you want me to go, I will." He came to a halt; there was nothing left to say.

Mona listened to his words with her head bowed, looking at the kitchen floor. As he stopped speaking, she lifted her head and looked him in the eye once more. There was no sign of any tenderness or forgiveness there, only the same degree of hurt and bitterness. When she spoke, there was a malevolence in her tone that he had never heard before. It shocked him. "Get out, you filthy pervert. Go and stick your prick up your boyfriend's arse, if that's what you want. Get out of this house now and never come back. You're dead to me from now on, David Edgeley."

David flinched but Mona took no notice. She pushed past him and rushed upstairs in floods of tears.

He stood there, uncertain what to do. His conscience told him that he should stay here and try to fix this; his common sense told him that fixing it was now impossible and that he should get out. His heart ached for Alan and to be held safe in his arms.

Eventually he moved slowly towards the back door and into the garden, which he had tended so avidly over the years, telling himself that it was his pride and joy. He looked round it now in the half light of a late summer evening, devastated by the speed at which events had moved.

He had been horrified at the nature and depth of Mona's reaction, but he had to recognise that he was the cause of it. She was right: his weakness and cowardice in not acknowledging his feelings and his love for Alan six years ago had been the root cause of the problem. He had been lying to himself as well as everybody else.

Christ, what a fucking mess. Uncertain of what to do, he sat on the bench in the back garden. He looked at his watch; it was just gone nine. He wondered if there was a train back to London tonight, but no, he'd have missed the last one. He could – in fact he *ought* – to go and see his parents but he couldn't face them tonight, not now. He'd go and see Jen. He could sleep on his sister's sofa tonight, see his parents tomorrow and then go to London. Except that Alan was away on this bloody course all week. Shit.

He pulled out his mobile to ring his sister. It turned out that she was with his parents, giving him no option but to go and see them. He called a cab to take him to his parents' house, and re-entered the house. His overnight bag from the London trip was still in the hall so he grabbed it and headed out of the front door for what would probably be the last time.

Chapter 34

Alan

After their exchange of text messages, Alan was the personification of a cat on a hot tin roof. He wished he smoked because at least it would keep his hands occupied. He poured himself a glass of wine and moved from the kitchen into the sitting room upstairs.

He switched the television on but was unable to concentrate; he couldn't have done even if he had been in the mood for frivolous Saturday night entertainment, which he certainly wasn't. He decided to listen to some music but stared at his CD collection for several minutes without being able to choose a suitable disc.

It occurred to him that he could do something practical with his time, so he went into his bedroom to get a load of dirty laundry. Downstairs in the kitchen, he found himself staring out of the window again; ten minutes had passed, during which he had been turning the laundry in his hands, creating a knotted mess which he had to untangle. He shook himself, put the washing into the machine and started it.

He remembered that he had left his phone upstairs. He raced up the single flight and grabbed the handset. Nothing.

Pacing about the room, he paused every now and again to look out of the front window into the street below. There was hardly anybody about – but then a lone figure passed under one of the lamp standards, his footsteps echoing against the tall terraced houses on either side of the street. The stranger seemed to have the same build as David, and Alan imagined briefly that it was actually him walking up the street, coming to the flat as he had in recent weeks. He'd be ready to kiss hello and say "hi" before settling down for an evening's cuddling in front of an old film. The figure passed on down the street, ending the brief illusion. It was not going to happen – at least not tonight, anyway. But would it ever happen again? Would David ever be in is arms once more? If so, when? And how?

Alan closed his eyes and fought back his tears. For at least the tenth time that day, he cursed the fact that this week of all weeks he had to do this sodding residential course in the middle of nowhere. The venue was remote enough to force him to travel tomorrow night to be there for the start of the course. He was committed to his job, and to the firm which had looked after him so well, but he did rather resent losing his Sunday. And, as it had turned out, it was spectacularly bad timing.

But his boss had been insistent. They had to be completely switched on to social media marketing; you couldn't simply rely on the geeky technical guys who understood all that stuff. Account managers and creative directors had to get a grip with it as well if future campaigns and pitches for accounts were going to reflect current marketplace trends adequately.

Alan understood the point completely and had been looking forward to the challenge – but then Friday night had happened and the whole weekend had turned to shit. He ran his hands through his hair distractedly. He should be with David and he couldn't be.

What the fuck is happening to him?

Tears welled up again, this time of both frustration and sympathy, and he headed into the kitchen to get another drink. He was in the kitchen when he felt his phone vibrate and heard the ping of an incoming message. It was a text.

DAVID:>> Total shitstorm at home. Mona threw me out. On way to mum and dad. Talk later.

Alan stared at the screen, horrified. He immediately hit the dial button – he needed to talk, to find out more, to see how the poor devil felt. It went straight to voicemail. Alan was frustrated but not surprised.

He tried to keep the agitation out of his voice as he left a message. "Hey, Davy. Just saw your text – wanted to make sure you were okay. Give me a call as soon as you can, love."

And to make sure, he also texted back.

ALAN:>> Really sorry, Davy. Hope you're OK. Anything I can do? Ring me as soon as you can. Love you Al.

Veering off Course

Chapter 35

David

The cab dropped him at his parents' house across the town around half an hour later. His sister Jen greeted him at the door, her face full of anxiety as she embraced him. "I'm so sorry, David love. Was it awful?"

He nodded whilst still wrapped in her arms, meaning that she felt rather than saw his response. Recovering a little, he lifted his head and spoke. "It was horrid, Jen. Much worse than I thought it would be. What about here?"

"Not good. Mum would be okay, I think, but Dad is not happy. I don't think he understands. They're both very worried about the boys."

David grunted. "I can well understand that. So am I."

"Anyway, go and freshen up, then come down and talk to them. But don't expect an easy ride."

He trod wearily upstairs to the bathroom and stripped off his uniform jacket and shirt. He looked at his clothes in surprise, suddenly remembering that he hadn't even had time to change before the shit had hit the fan. As he washed himself down, he replayed the scene with Mona, her words reverberating through his mind. Whatever pressure might be put on him in the next hour or two, he knew that the split with his wife was irrevocable. Things had been said tonight, positions taken, from which there was no going back. He would try to get on with her in whatever way, shape or form she would allow, for the sake of his boys, his parents. But that would be the extent of their future relationship. And he had a shrewd suspicion that she would not allow very much, if anything.

He dried himself off. He felt better for the wash, though he would have given his eye teeth for a long hot shower before falling into bed – ideally with Alan, but even alone would be good. He felt so tired, as if he'd not rested at all since that moment outside the pub on Friday night.

Remembering Alan, he pulled his mobile out, only to see a blank screen. The battery had run out. Shit. He must remember to plug it in and contact him soon, then charge it overnight.

He dressed again and prepared to head downstairs to face his next ordeal: a discussion with his parents.

✥

David sat in his parents' lounge, accompanied by his sister. Because he was the baby of the family, having been a late unplanned addition, there was a wide age gap between him and his parents. George Enderby had been almost forty when David was born and was now in his late sixties. The age gap had been widened by George's conservative outlook on life; he had always been resistant to change. Consequently, he remained wrapped up in the moral and ethical approaches that he had known as a boy in the 1940s.

David had dreaded this conversation for weeks – and being outed by his own trade-union chairman was hardly likely to make the discussion any easier.

"I'm sorry that I didn't get a chance to talk to you before all this started. It must have been a bit of a shock for you."

"Yes, it was, love," replied his mother. "But I understand that it was difficult for you too."

"It was a lot to come to terms with, seeing Alan again and bringing everything back."

David looked at this father. Definitely not happy. He remained silent as David told his side of the story and the expression on his face stayed closed, as if he were hiding his true reactions behind shutters. Now, he spoke. "Yes, it's all very unfortunate. I can understand that you might have problems with urges. Lots of people do – but they control them. Why do you have to act on them?"

David was thrown by the question, which had never occurred to him. "Because this is me, Dad. I didn't choose to be born like this, it happened. I didn't choose my sexuality."

"But that's what I don't get, David lad. You claim not to have a choice, and yet six years ago you did seem to have a choice and you chose to get married. You made certain promises to Mona and went on to father a couple of children. As far as I'm concerned, you ought to keep those promises." He paused. "After all, liking other men is nothing to be proud of, is it? It certainly wasn't in my day. People controlled their urges when I was a boy, dealt with them in other ways. Urges are not an excuse for breaking promises, David. Not a reason for failing in your duty."

"Dad, David made a mistake six years ago," Jennifer intervened. David shot her a grateful look. "Surely he can't be expected to pay for that for the rest of his life?"

Their father shook his head. The set of his jaw made it clear that he was not going to budge. The whole family knew that look: a granite-like obstinacy took over, after which he was unshakeable.

He spoke again. "We love you as parents should, David, and we will carry on doing that. But we can't welcome you into our home for as long as this goes on. You need to give up the London job, stop seeing Alan, and make it up with Mona for the sake of boys. For our sake too."

"And what about my sake, Dad?"

"You made your bed six years ago, David. As far as I am concerned, it's your duty now to lie on it, and to honour the promises you made."

"I can't do that, Dad. I'm sorry. I know I've done wrong and I'm willing to work as hard as I can to atone for that. But I cannot live a complete lie. Even if Mona was prepared to forgive me, to allow me back into the house – which I very much doubt – going back from here wouldn't be fair to her, to the boys or to me. In fact, it would quite possibly do more harm than good for the boys to grow up in such an atmosphere."

His father's jaw remained immovable. "I'm sorry, David, I think you're wrong. Children brought up in a stable household, with two parents, almost always do better."

"But number one, it would not be a stable household.

And number two, it's not the case where the parents don't get on or actively dislike each other."

"But you *do* get on, and quite well too from what your mother and I have always seen."

"That was then, Dad, and this is now. You should have heard Mona's language tonight. As I said, I don't think she'd have me back even if I wanted to go."

"You can argue all you like, David, but my mind is made up. You are not welcome in this house while you're in this state. I think you'd better leave."

Jennifer let out a gasp of horror. "Dad! You can't mean it! Your own son. She threw *him* out!"

Her father rose from his chair and prepared to leave the room. "I've nothing more to say. And I wish you'd stop your interfering, Jennifer."

He went out and they heard his tread on the stairs. This was the cue for their mother to break down. Her tears flowed as she tried to apologise to both of them at once and tell them to take no notice. Their dad would come round, she was sure. "I'll go and put the kettle on," she concluded, and fled for the kitchen.

David stayed where he was for a few moments, struggling to come to terms with his father's words, and – worse – the coldness of his manner. Jennifer looked at him. "Stay where you are, David. You can stay with Mark and me tonight. Let me see to Mum. I'll only be a minute."

The sound of her voice awoke David from his reverie and he looked up at her. He shook his head. "Thanks, Jen, but I need to get away. Now. Tonight. I'll be in touch soon." He picked up his bag and went towards the front door.

Jennifer shouted after him not to be stupid then rose to

follow him, calling him back. She ran to the front door as he left through the gate. She shook her head and threw up her arms in despair as he set off down the road. She couldn't catch him and her mother needed her. She turned back and went inside the house.

David moved along the road at a brisk pace, still feeling the sting of his father's rejection. Gradually he accelerated into a jog. All he was aware of was a need to get away from Yorkshire as soon as possible and to find sanctuary with Alan.

With a flat battery in his phone, he was unable to contact anybody. His fury with his father might have propelled him out of the house and up to the end of his parents' road, but what to do now? He glanced up the hill, the huge floodlit directional sign looming above him against the night sky. It acted as a reminder that he was almost next to the motorway junction. What if he could hitch a ride to London? It was too late for a bus or train but, if he was lucky, he could still be at Alan's for the morning, to see him before he had to leave for his course. That would be the best thing ever.

A distant alarm bell rang in the back of his mind about the risks of hitch-hiking, of being assaulted by some weirdo, but he shook his head to clear it. He'd be all right. After all that had happened to him tonight, surely nothing else would go wrong.

As he headed towards the roundabout, he heard a car behind him. Purely on the off-chance, he stuck out his thumb in the time-honoured way. A car passed him and, to his utter astonishment, pulled up a few yards ahead of him. He jogged up to the passenger side and looked inside.

"How far are you going, mate?" said a voice with a pronounced London accent.

David did a quick assessment of the driver – mid-thirties probably, shirt sleeves and chinos. Looked okay, and the car was okay too, a modern Audi.

"I was hoping to get to London."

"Well, it's your lucky night. Hop in, mate."

Veering off Course

Chapter 36

Alan

As the minutes ticked by and there was still no word from David, Alan grew increasingly worried. His fear was enhanced by his sense of powerlessness and dislocation. Whereas previous generations had lived with the limitations of the post, telegrams and landline telephones, life had now changed beyond recognition. Earlier constraints had been swept away, and instant communication was the new norm – whether by mobile, e-mail or text message. Delays in hearing from people or getting responses from them had therefore become that much more stressful.

Time passed, but agonisingly slowly. He spent the minutes between looking at his phone to see if he had missed a call or a text, and worrying about the hypothetical situations his imagination was constantly creating. Adding to his frustration was the fact that there was nobody else he could contact. He had David's home number but, since he had received that one brief text message, Alan knew that home was the one place David would not be. After a moment, he had an inspiration – Jennifer. He was sure that he had written down some contact information for David's sister and her husband the other week, after David had come out to them.

He went to his desk and scrabbled amongst his papers, eventually finding the note that he had made. There was a name – presumably Jen's husband's surname – and an address, but no landline or mobile numbers. Eventually, it struck him that, given a name and an address, he could at least get a landline number from directory enquiries.

Five minutes later, he was dialling a Sedgethwaite number with trembling fingers, hoping against hope that he could find out what was going on. The ring tone sounded for an awfully long time, and Alan was about to give up when his call was answered.

"Mark Hudson."

"Oh hi. Sorry to disturb you. My name is Alan Foreshaw and..."

"You're David's boyfriend," said the friendly voice at the other end. "How can I help, Alan?"

That was a good start. He sounded really helpful.

"Yeah, that's right. I'm a bit worried about him, to be honest. I had a short text a while ago saying that his wife had thrown him out and he was headed for his parents' house, but I haven't heard a word since and I'm getting a bit frantic."

"I'm afraid I can't tell you much more, Alan. I know that Jen is with her mum and dad now, so if David's headed there he'll be in good company."

"Oh, I see. That's comforting anyway. It's just so hard being this far away, y'know?"

"I can well understand. This is a difficult time for you

all, I'm sure. I'll make sure that Jen rings you when she gets in, or David if she brings him too. I'd better take your number."

They went through the formalities of exchanging contact information and ended the call. Alan felt a little better for knowing that somebody up there seemed to have David's back. He could at least relax a little in the knowledge that he would hear from somebody soon.

Suddenly, his phone pinged with a text. He reached for his mobile eagerly, fumbling in his agitation, almost dropping it. Surely this would be news from David. He slumped with disappointment when he saw Simon's name on the display.

SIMON:>> There's a lot of pacing about going on up there. You okay?

ALAN:>> No. Come up and keep me company?

SIMON:>> Sure – give us two minutes.

Within two minutes, there was a tap on David's front door. There stood Peter and Simon, bottle and glasses in hand, anxious looks on their faces.

"We thought you might need relief supplies," explained Simon with a grin. "Now tell us what the fuck is going on."

Alan told them the story as far as he knew it.

"So, she threw him out after all," was Simon's response. "You know, the awful thing is that, seeing things from her point of view, I can hardly blame her."

This earned him a glare from Peter. "Simon, love, so not helping."

Simon blushed and took refuge in a sip of his wine. "Oh, sorry."

"It's a discussion we need to have," acknowledged Alan, "but probably not now. Anyway, the point is that he texted me and that was nearly two hours ago, when he was on the way to his parents. There's been nothing since. I just wish he'd let me know."

"You know his parents, don't you? How do you think they will have reacted?"

"He's the baby of the family so he's always been loved, especially by his mum. Dad's a bit austere and old-fashioned, and they'll definitely hate all the rumours and gossip. The short answer is I don't know. But I'm worried, especially by how David might react if anything went wrong."

"Christ," said Simon, half to himself. "The poor love."

There was silence in the room; all three were lost briefly in their own memories of a coming-out experience. The sound of an incoming call on Alan's mobile broke the silence, the ringtone jarring and making them all jump. Alan reached across and answered it.

"Alan? Alan Foreshaw?"

"Yeah, hi. Who's calling?"

"This is Jennifer. Jennifer Hudson, David's sister?"

"Er, hi, Jennifer. Thanks very much for calling. I'm very worried."

"Have you not heard from him? David, I mean. I know you told Mark that you hadn't, but I thought I'd check."

"Why, Jennifer? What happened?"

"They threw him out as well, Alan. God, it was so awful, and he looked absolutely terrible. He ran off. I tried to stop him, but..." Her voice became shakier as she uttered the words, trailing off into a sob.

"Oh, Jen. Was it his dad?"

There was silence at the other end for a moment as David's sister gathered herself. When she spoke, her voice was steadier. "Yes, it was Dad. I was with them most of the day, keeping them company, reassuring them. Mum was upset at how it had happened, and cross with David for not telling them himself, but otherwise she was okay. Eventually I got her to see it from his point of view, and to accept the fact that he hadn't actually made up his mind what he was going to do."

"True. He was very worried about the boys."

"Yes, exactly what I said. Any road, she understood in the end. But Dad was very quiet all day and I couldn't get him to open up. He's very…" she hesitated, looking for the right words "…stiff upper lip."

"Yeah, bottles it up. Doesn't say much at all. He was always a bit like that when we were boys."

"As a result, I didn't know what to expect when David arrived."

"How was he?" interrupted Alan, anxiety making his voice sharper than he'd intended.

"A bit subdued but he seemed okay, especially after we got him to go upstairs and have a wash." She paused, letting out a long unsteady breath that was not quite a sigh. "Anyway, we sat down to talk. Mum was fine but Dad started on about giving in to 'urges', as he called them. Said he understood people got them, but they didn't have to act on them."

"Oh, God. Then what?"

"Basically, he told David that he'd made promises to Mona six years ago and he ought to keep them. And that he wouldn't be welcome in the house until he did."

"Christ, Jen. How did David take it?"

"He argued back at first, said that he didn't choose to be how he was ... gay or bi or whatever. But now he had to face up to it."

"And?"

David could almost hear the resigned shrug that Jen gave as she replied. "Dad said that David had had a choice six years ago. He'd made his bed and now he must lie on it." Her voice had taken on a flat tone as she said those words, but it quickly broke again. "God, Alan, I'll never forget the look on David's face when he said that. He looked so wrecked."

"I'm not surprised, poor devil. What happened next?"

Jen's voice resumed its flat tone as she replied. "Dad told him to go and stomped off upstairs. Mum dissolved into floods of tears and David got up and left. Alan, it was awful. I can't ever remember a night like it in our family."

Alan was relentless. Stuff sympathy, he had to *know*. "What then, Jen? What happened to Davy?"

"I asked him to wait, to come back with me to our house. I had to give Mum a few minutes, but he wouldn't. Wait, I mean. He ran out of the front door – I tried to stop him, but he was off down the road. I thought he'd be all right, that he'd ring you." Her voice wavered again.

"Bloody hell, Jen. I'm sorry you had to cope with all that. I should have been around to help."

"I don't know that there was much you could have done, Alan love."

"I could have been there for him."

Jennifer's practical side took over as she responded.

"That's as may be, but it doesn't make any difference now, does it?"

"S'pose not. It's just … I feel so powerless."

"I understand that, Alan. But what do we do now?"

"Call the police? Ring the hospitals? I don't know."

"Too soon to call the police, I think. Mark's here and we could ring the hospitals. Let's do that first." She sounded almost relieved at being able to take some practical steps. "I'll let you know how we get on," she said abruptly and rang off.

Peter occupied himself in pouring them more wine. Simon looked at Alan open-mouthed. "I heard virtually all that. Poor devil, I wonder how he must be feeling."

"I know, Si. I'm getting terrified now. He's not responding to texts or calls, and we don't know where he is. Shit."

Simon nodded. "I know, love. But I think he'll be okay. Underneath it all I think he's quite strong. He's always struck me as a level-headed sort of guy. Not one to do anything rash."

"I'd agree with you normally. But today he's been outed at work, thrown out of his home and rejected by his parents. Not exactly a formula for level-headedness, is it?"

Simon gave a small giggle despite himself. "No, when you put it like that…"

"Trouble is, I don't even know how or where to start looking for him."

Veering off Course

Chapter 37

David

The car was warm and comfortable. The driver, who introduced himself as Gavin, was a freelance photographer returning home after an assignment in Leeds. He explained that he hated hotels with a passion and preferred late-night driving when the roads were quieter.

David talked of his job and his kids, managing to hold up one end of a somewhat desultory conversation despite while feeling completely wrecked physically and emotionally. It occurred to him that talking about other subjects was quite a good way of distracting himself; it helped him avoid the need to think further about the events of the evening. He was fully aware that he would have to do so at some point, but was grateful to be able to postpone it, at least for a while.

Eventually, fatigue overtook him and David fell asleep in mid-sentence. Gavin, who had found him an engaging companion, shrugged, turned the music up slightly and remained silent.

When David awoke, an hour had passed and he was

aware that the signs had changed. Instead of South Yorkshire destinations like Rotherham and Sheffield, the signs were pointing towards the Midlands towns, Derby and Nottingham then Leicester and Birmingham.

"I'm sorry," he said. "Not very good company, am I?"

Gavin laughed gently. "Don't worry, mate. You must have needed it."

They passed a sign for a service area. "I need a pee," said Gavin. "Fancy a coffee?"

"Sounds good to me."

As they pulled in, David recognised Leicester Forest East, the usual venue for comfort breaks on his coach journeys.

Hot drinks in hand, they sat opposite one another in the coffee shop. David had his first sight of Gavin in normal light and saw a pair of friendly brown eyes looking at him from a square face topped with short-cropped brown hair. At that moment, the eyes were full of concern.

"Crikey, mate, you do look wrecked. No wonder you fell asleep. Are you okay?"

David gave a half-smile. "Not really – but getting better the further I get from Yorkshire."

"I'm sorry to pry, but you remind me of Ben at the end of term."

"Ben?" queried David.

"Sorry. My boyfriend. He's a special-needs teacher in London. He's absolutely wrecked at the end of every term – literally grey with fatigue. You looked just like that a minute ago."

"Boyfriend?"

"Yeah, I'm gay." Gavin narrowed his eyes. "That bother

you?" he asked with a slight edge to his tone.

"No, no. God no. Sorry, I hadn't thought, that's all. You didn't seem…"

"The type? Is there a type, do you think?" Again, there was a slight edge to his voice.

"Again, no. Christ, I am making a mess of this, aren't I? Sorry. Let's wind back a bit. The main point is: me too."

"Oh, okay. My turn to be a bit surprised. Did you not mention kids earlier? I assumed…"

David gave a small chuckle. "Yeah, so did I. That's the problem." He'd intended to continue, but his own words brought him up short. He'd never thought of it like that before. He *had* assumed. And that *had* been his problem. He couldn't explain why that made him feel slightly better, but it did. By mutual consent, they moved from the cafeteria back towards Gavin's car. Neither spoke, but somehow it was a comfortable silence.

"Care to elaborate?" Gavin's gentle question brought David out of his thoughts.

"Six years ago, I … er … hooked up with my oldest friend on his last night at home before he moved to London. I panicked, got married and was resolutely straight." He paused. Put like that it all sounded very bald – a logical sequence of events that had not been logical at all. Or, strictly speaking, a sequence. "As I told you, Mona – that's my wife – and I had the two boys. Everything was fine. Until it wasn't. I was bored, fed-up and – I now realise – lonely."

"Yeah, been there. Done that. Got the T-shirt."

David let out another short laugh. "Anyway, in February, up pops my old school friend again. Long story short, we went out for a drink and I kissed him. Suddenly I understood."

"Oh, David," said Gavin sadly. "I'm afraid I know what's coming."

"Yeah. I started driving coaches to London instead of buses to Leeds, staying with him on the overnight duties. Best of both worlds, you know? Trying to work out what the fuck I was going to do."

"I can imagine. How to find the words to tell her?"

"Got it in one. Not only her, of course, but parents, parents-in-law, people at work ... the whole bloody world. And terrified of course."

"At what people would say. Yeah, I know. And?"

"Anyway, fate took a hand. Alan and I were in the West End last night." David paused again as images of the previous evening flashed before his eyes. *Christ, was it only last night?* "We were spotted, by a work colleague – the union chairman, actually. Not one of my fans."

"Ah."

"Yeah, so I've been outed at work, thrown out by my wife and rejected by my dad – all in one shit-fest of a day."

"Fuuuuck, David. And you're still in one piece?"

Another short laugh escaped him. "Yeah, just about holding it together, thanks."

Except that became the moment he wasn't. It was as if the recital of this abbreviated version of the story opened a sluice gate, allowing all the pent-up feelings of the day to flood out. Tears started to flow down David's face, silently at first as he struggled to control his feelings, but soon accompanied by deep sobs.

Gavin reached across the central console with his spare

hand to offer comfort, patting David's thigh. David was grateful for the warmth of that small amount of human contact.

"Do you want to stop again?" Gavin asked gently.

This prompted David to recover himself a little. "No, no. I'll be okay. It's very late and you want to get home."

They were silent for a few moments before David spoke again. "I'm sorry about all that. Telling you the story brought it all back."

"Yeah, made it seem real again. I get that. What now though? You're heading for Alan's place, I assume?"

"Yeah. I just wanted to be with him, after ... y'know."

"Does he know you're coming?"

David shook his head in the dark. "No, my battery died before I could ring him. Haven't had the chance since."

Gavin laughed. "Do you mean to say that you've been in this car for nearly two hours and you haven't asked to borrow the phone? Or used the public booths at the services?"

David looked at Gavin across the car in horror. Gavin, glancing momentarily to his left, caught the expression on David's face in the light of a streetlamp and laughed. "Dear me, the mobile-phone generation. What have we come to?"

Gavin reached across and placed his mobile phone in David's hand. "Go on, ring him. Can't offer you any privacy, I'm afraid. But at least you can put him out of his misery. The poor guy will be frantic, I expect. We should be in London around three-thirty. Where does he live?"

"Clapham."

"Oh, fine. We're in Balham. So tell him I'll drop you

off."

David laughed. "Do you actually exist or were you sent from heaven?"

Chapter 38

Alan

Alan was half asleep when his phone rang. Simon and Peter had stayed with him for a couple of hours, trying to keep him calm and distracting him by talking about pretty much everything under the sun. Eventually, though, the conversation dried up. Simon, in particular, looked exhausted because he had been working all day. Alan had packed them off downstairs, promising faithfully to let them both know when there was any news.

Alone again, he spent some time thinking deliberately happy thoughts – how this crisis betokened a major shift in the life that he and David hoped to build together. It ended the period of limbo while David hesitated about what to do and tried to pluck up the courage to tell Mona what was going on. Well, she sure as hell knew now.

His thoughts shifted and he felt slightly guilty for feeling even the tiniest bit glad about the crisis. What horror David must have gone through tonight – outed at work, the row with Mona and finally his dad's rejection. Goodness knows what this would have done to his self-confidence; it was never his strong suit at the best of times.

It dawned on Alan once more that his concerns, and hopes for the future, were all very fine and nice but were not a lot of good as long as he had no idea where the fuck David was. And so he began a whole new cycle of worry and fear: worry about David's safety, and fear that he, Alan, would lose him again from his life. That would be the ultimate cruelty after missing him for all those years.

The whole process left him exhausted and drained the last of his energy; his eyelids started to droop. At that point, his phone rang. The number on his screen was an unknown one but nonetheless he took the call ... and it was then that he heard a familiar voice asking if that was Al.

✦

Of necessity their call was brief, since they could say little more in such circumstances once they'd established the central fact that David was okay and would be at the Clapham flat in around ninety minutes.

Though Alan was pissed with him for taking the risk of hitching a lift, David seemed to have fallen on his feet and his imminent arrival was a terrific bonus. He stayed looking at his phone for several minutes after the call ended, a slow smile spreading across his face and a warm glow spreading through his body.

He realised that he had things to do. Despite the lateness of the hour, he needed to reassure Jennifer that her brother was safe and sound, as well as letting Simon and Peter know. He rang the former and texted the latter, reasoning that if they were already asleep they would at least get to know as soon as they woke up.

Jennifer was mightily relieved to get Alan's call, and was even more horrified at the idea of David hitching a lift. They discussed the fallout of the night's events and agreed to keep in close touch. Like Alan, she was nervous about the effect that the day's events would have on her baby brother, but she said more than once that she was sure Alan would look after him properly. "You always took such care of each other when you were boys. I often think of that, and how jealous I was as a teenager. I so wanted to have somebody like that in my life."

"But you met Mark eventually. He came along in the end."

By the time he had finished his call to Jen, there was less than an hour to go before David was due to arrive. He had time for a quick shower if he got a shift on, which would freshen him up after a sweaty and unsatisfactory evening, rinsing away the worries and stomach-wrenching fear that he had been experiencing all day.

Veering off Course

Chapter 39

David

The phone call out of the way, David felt more relaxed than he had done for weeks. He glanced across at his companion. He could see enough of his face in the streetlights as they drove south to see a faint smile on his lips.

"Thanks very much for letting me make the call, Gavin. That was great."

"He was relieved?"

"You could say that."

"It sounds as if you're very close. That's good."

"We've known each other since we were nine. I don't suppose there are many surprises now."

Gavin laughed. "No, I suppose you're right. Does that worry you?"

"A lack of surprises? God, no. It was always us against the world. The only time life felt wrong for me was during the six years when we were apart. I realised that as soon as I caught sight of him getting on my bus in Leeds last February."

"You're very lucky, you know. To have that sort of

connection with anybody."

"I know. It's going to help a lot over the coming months."

"So how do you see the future?"

"To be honest, I don't think either of us has got that far. We've talked about me moving to London, getting a driving job – maybe even going to college. But we've no definite plans. It all seemed like an impossible dream."

"Sure. Dreaming about a future is important, but it doesn't always help with the steering."

"I'm not with you."

"Sorry, I get a bit cryptic sometimes. Ben gets cross with me when I do it. My brain gets ahead of me."

"Right, I understand. So what's this about steering?"

"I meant that it's good to have dreams, to have an object to work towards. We all need that. But in the end, most of our energies are taken up with simply steering the ship – keeping everything on course with our lives, despite the shit that happens. To survive, we have to navigate our way round everything that threatens to impede us."

David laughed. "I understand you now. Yes, I think you're right. And being a driver, I know a bit about the need to steer straight."

It was Gavin's turn to laugh. "I should hope you do."

"Still, I like the words. Navigating our way through life. Must remember to tell Al about that."

They were quiet for a while. Looking across quickly, Gavin realised that David had drifted off again. The light from an overhead gantry caught his face; much of the pain he had seen at the service area earlier had been erased.

He smiled. Ben would be proud of him.

✛

By the time David woke again, they were leaving the motorway and moving in to London's northern suburbs. At this time of night, there was nothing to be gained by using the North Circular, so Gavin headed straight through the centre of the city. David watched in awe as they traversed streets still unfamiliar to him, crossing Blackfriars Bridge with its spectacular views and then turning to run alongside the river towards Vauxhall and on to Clapham. Gavin pointed out St Thomas's Hospital to their right and Lambeth Palace to their left, before directing David's gaze back to the right, to the famous view across the river to the Houses of Parliament.

As they neared Alan's flat, David felt his stomach muscles tighten. Whether it was from nerves or anticipation, he wasn't sure.

After a longish silence, Gavin spoke. "Thanks for the company tonight, David, mate. It was great to meet you."

"It's me who should do the thanking. I'm so grateful for the ride – and everything else. You've been great. I'd like to stay in touch and to meet Ben some time."

"Yeah, I'd like that too. You can never have too many friends in this bloody city. Especially gay ones."

David laughed. "I don't know yet – I suppose I'm about to find out."

"Yeah, well, take it from one who knows."

They exchanged numbers. Suddenly they were there, at the end of Alan's road.

"You can drop me here, if you like. Save turning round."

"Sure, thanks. Don't be a stranger, David. Keep in

touch."

It was awkward. David felt he couldn't simply get out of the car. He held out his hand for a shake but found himself being pulled gently across the central console into an awkward sideways hug. It felt good, especially when he got a kiss as well. It was on the lips but somehow very chaste.

Gavin winked at him as they pulled apart. "Don't forget the navigation, mate. Keeping the steering true."

"Will do."

David left the car, stretching himself as he stood on the pavement. Gavin accelerated away and was gone. David turned and walked up the road towards the flat.

Chapter 40

Alan

Showered and refreshed, Alan returned to his front room and stood at the window once again. He looked out along the street recalling his earlier vigil, dreaming of a time when he'd see David walking along, heading for the flat.

Now, with a speed that almost took his breath away, events meant that the dream was about to be fulfilled. The chances were that the very next person he saw walking up the street would be him. His Davy, his friend, and soulmate. The love of his life.

He closed his eyes, overwhelmed by the thought. Now they could plan their life together. He knew there'd be a lot to face over the next few months, especially for David with a divorce and possible custody battle, not to mention the challenges of a new job and a new city. But he was absolutely sure that it would, in the end, be worth it.

As he opened his eyes again, he caught movement through the leaves of a tree. A figure moved into clear sight. It was him.

Oblivious to the fact that it was gone three in the

morning, Alan raced down the stairs and threw open the front door of the building as David came through the gate and turned onto the path.

David grinned. "Hey."

They came together in a bone-crushing hug.

"Welcome home, Davy."

"Thanks, Al. Good to be here."

To be continued.

Veering off Course

Acknowledgements

My grateful thanks to my editor Karen Holmes, beta reader Kirsten Waite and cover designer Hilary Pitts for their hard work in helping to bring this book to market.
My deepest thanks also to my husband Michael Anderson and to all my friends for their help and encouragement over the last few months.

About the Author

Chris Cheek was born and brought up in South London. He has strong family ties with northern England and is a graduate of Lancaster University. He and his husband, Michael, have been together for forty years and have lived in the Yorkshire Dales since 1994.

This is Chris's third novel. His first book, *The Stamp of Nature*, was published in June 2018. The second, *A Year of Awakening*, followed in October 2018.

He writes a regular blog which can be found at www.chrischeek.me.

Lightning Source UK Ltd.
Milton Keynes UK
UKHW042203240219
337902UK00005B/108/P